If Ian couldn't break that window, he and Makenzie would die in seconds...

All their assailants had to do was spray the room with bullets and it would all be over.

"I'm covering the door." Makenzie dropped to one knee to take aim away from the door's direct line of sight.

Ian hefted the bat and swung close to the bottom corner. The window shattered in a hail of shards.

The door burst open, crashing against the wall. Someone rushed into the room.

Makenzie fired—and a male grunted and staggered backward.

He didn't go down. The shadowy figure charged forward. From the way the guy moved, it was terrifyingly clear...

He was armored up. No amount of shooting was going to permanently stop him or his buddies, either.

Another shadow entered and jerked Makenzie backward. Her gun clattered to the hardwood floor.

Jodie Bailey writes novels about freedom and the heroes who fight for it. Her novel *Crossfire* won a 2015 RT Reviewers' Choice Best Book Award. She is convinced a camping trip to the beach with her family, a good cup of coffee and a great book can cure all ills. Jodie lives in North Carolina with her husband, her daughter and two dogs.

Books by Jodie Bailey

Love Inspired Suspense

Dead Run
Calculated Vendetta
Fatal Response
Mistaken Twin
Hidden Twin
Canyon Standoff
"*Missing in the Wilderness*"
Fatal Identity
Under Surveillance
Captured at Christmas
Witness in Peril
Blown Cover

Alaska K-9 Unit

Deadly Cargo

Rocky Mountain K-9 Unit

Defending from Danger

Visit the Author Profile page at LoveInspired.com.

BLOWN COVER

JODIE BAILEY

LOVE INSPIRED SUSPENSE
INSPIRATIONAL ROMANCE

LOVE INSPIRED®SUSPENSE
INSPIRATIONAL ROMANCE

ISBN-13: 978-1-335-58872-2

Recycling programs
for this product may
not exist in your area.

Blown Cover

Love Inspired
22 Adelaide St. West, 41st Floor
Toronto, Ontario M5H 4E3, Canada
www.LoveInspired.com

Printed in U.S.A.

And she called the name of the Lord that spake unto her,
Thou God seest me: for she said, Have I also here
looked after him that seeth me?
—*Genesis* 16:13

To Mrs. Cook
God saw me...
And so did you

ONE

Darkness lurked in the shadows of Christmas tree lights and white tapered candles. Sinister. Deadly.

Special Agent Makenzie Fuller could almost feel it.

If only she could *see* it.

The bride and groom twirled beneath the raw beam ceiling of the ballroom at Hunter's Ridge Castle. The venue in the North Carolina Blue Ridge Mountains was warm and romantic, as elegantly dressed guests danced the night away and toasted the happy couple.

The air seemed to buzz with a different vibe entirely.

Makenzie had felt this kind of hum against her skin in the past, shortly before her first partner was found dead, executed by an international arms dealer.

Shortly before her second partner vanished in a hail of accusations.

Backing closer to a massive Christmas tree wrapped in white lights, Makenzie attempted to ease the tension from her posture, to look as though she was enjoying the reception.

She wasn't. Did the bride realize her Uncle Robert's lavish gift of a Christmas wedding in a mountain castle had been funded by blood money?

Makenzie took in a deep breath and exhaled slowly. If she looked as ill-at-ease as she felt, her nerves could unravel everything that nearly a year's worth of undercover work had painstakingly knit together. It had taken months to earn Robert Butler's trust. More months to work her way into his confidence as his personal bodyguard. She didn't need him questioning her loyalty or her readiness, not when he was close to making the deal that could nail him to the wall, revealing the final proof that he was the mastermind behind a series of arms thefts from military bases across the southern United States.

A transaction that could put them on the trail of another arms dealer, possibly an even bigger fish than Butler himself.

Once he did, Makenzie could have her life back. Be herself again. Maybe even see her family for Christmas. She needed space to detox from being deep undercover within hours of home. Time to process the way Ian Andrews had run out on her and on their team. How could—

"We have a problem." The low voice at her elbow nearly made her jump.

Only training kept her steady. She dipped her chin to the side, bringing her ear closer to Robert Butler where he'd slipped up beside her. "What can I do?" She kept her voice low, playing the part of his ever-trustworthy, ever-capable protector.

He had no idea her singular goal was to watch his empire fall.

"Keep an eye out." Wearing a white tuxedo jacket and black pants, his attire coordinated perfectly with her formal white pantsuit and flowing black overlay. Holding two champagne flutes, the silver-haired gentleman looked every inch the doting rich uncle.

Few people in the room knew he was a ruthless killer.

He sipped regally from his champagne, offering Makenzie the second glass.

She shook her head. "Not while I'm on the job."

With a slight smile, he signaled a passing waiter, settled his empty glass on the tray and held the one he'd offered her. He eyed the crowd casually but, from experience, Makenzie knew his shrewd gaze could see whatever disturbance had her skin crawling.

He glanced at her and smiled. Ostensibly, she was his date for the evening. He preferred not to let his family know that his criminal activities required someone to watch his back.

Funny how evil men often wanted those closest to them to believe they were perfect.

Stepping closer, he turned, his chest grazing her biceps. When his breath brushed her ear, it took every ounce of her training not to pull away. She'd repeatedly told him she never mixed business with pleasure, claiming it would rob her of her edge.

For months, he'd played by her rules. He'd better not start bending them tonight.

"There's a traitor in the room." His champagne-scented whisper almost punched the air from her lungs. The only agency investigating Robert Butler was her military investigative unit, Eagle Overwatch.

She was the only undercover agent on the case. In Robert Butler's eyes, *traitor* would certainly apply.

She managed not to tense. *Breathe. Don't let him know he rattled you.*

Makenzie furrowed her brows and reset her thinking into character. Her life depended on it. "That's impossible, Robert. I vetted the guest list myself."

Stepping in front of her, Butler blocked her view of the ballroom as well as her avenue of escape. He leaned in, his dark words hot against her cheek. "The guy's been working with a possible future associate of mine, but as it turns out, he might not be...aboveboard."

It took everything she had not to openly groan. How had this slipped past her? No names on the guest list had matched up to any watch list.

Criminal or not, she couldn't stand by while Butler took a life.

"Point him out and I'll handle it." That was her "job," after all. She could take the person into custody and get him out of harm's way without blowing her cover or getting an outlier killed. Her team might even be able to offer a deal for testimony against Butler or his *associate*. "I'll—"

"No. This one's personal. The guy's looking to double-cross someone I'm especially interested in protecting."

Her heart beat faster. Could the *someone* be the person he was meeting tonight? While she was out to connect Butler to weapons thefts, he'd been hinting at meeting with a big player, an international dealer who went by the code name Storm. Storm had recently given him a laptop, likely to communicate more securely. She was itching to access it. "How do you know?"

"I have people besides you who provide me with information." He stood taller, finally exiting her personal space. "It's been a while since I got my hands dirty. You stay and make sure no one disrupts Emma's wedding. I'll return before they cut the cake." He lifted her hand and slipped his champagne glass into it. "You stay here. I want you in my meeting." He offered a slight smile. "My associate would like to meet you." He was gone, striding across the floor before Makenzie could react.

She gripped the flute so tightly it was a shock the crystal didn't shatter. She tapped her foot. Being in that meeting could bring more intel than she'd ever dreamed.

It would mean obeying him to the letter. Standing by while he killed a man.

She couldn't do that.

If she interfered, Butler would wonder why. His whole organization would. The cover it had taken nearly twelve months to build would shatter like the glass in her hand.

She could alert the local police, but if this was a test of her loyalty ahead of his meeting, she'd be dead and the investigation would fall apart.

The only person who could handle this was her.

Slipping through the crowd, Makenzie trailed Butler. She threaded her way around the fringes of the dance floor, avoiding Butler's half-dozen minions stationed around the room. Most wouldn't question her authority, but a couple were still burned that he'd chosen a woman for her position. They wouldn't hesitate to cast suspicion on her.

If they hadn't already.

As Butler stepped outside, Makenzie kept close to the floor-to-ceiling windows, following his path.

He strode across a large stone-walled balcony toward a group of men chatting in the brittle moonlight, approaching a dark blond man whose back was to Makenzie.

She leaned closer to the window. Something about him was—

"What are you doing?" The gruff voice was followed by a rough shove to her shoulder. "Butler said he was handling this."

Great. Cale Nicholson was over six feet of former college linebacker brutality who fully believed he should be the man in Makenzie's shoes.

She shot him a withering look. *Take the offensive. Throw him off-balance.* "Protecting the boss. What are *you* doing?" How could she get him off her scent without raising suspicion?

Looking straight down his nose from nearly a foot above her, Nicholson stepped closer, almost backing her into a stand of glowing Christmas trees. "He told you to watch the guests."

More and more, this felt like she was being tested…or outed.

Feigning annoyance, she crossed her arms and held his gaze. "I'm making sure the walk-away goes as planned, as ordered by the boss. Surely you saw us talking by the Christmas tree on the other side of the room?"

Doubt flitted across Nicholson's features, but he squared his shoulders in defiance of it...and of her.

Makenzie glanced out the window. Butler had guided the man away from the group and was headed for an arched walkway that led to the parking lot.

This was not good. And she was stuck in a muscle-flexing match with an ego-bruised macho man.

With a flash of inspiration, Makenzie stepped closer to Nicholson. "What will he say when I tell him you walked away from your post by the gifts?" She crowded him until he backed down. "If even one cof-fee maker walks out of here while you're challenging my authority, I will make cer-tain your next job involves scrubbing toi-lets. Are we clear?"

Nicholson almost bowed up to her again but, with a sneer that promised trouble later, he stalked away.

There was no time for relief. As soon as

Nicholson was out of sight, she eased to the window, peeking through the sheer curtains.

Butler was nearly to her position, his arm around the shoulder of the man he'd approached. His body blocked her view of the victim, but it was clear Butler had managed to drug his prey. He was known for incapacitating before killing.

Coward.

She had to stop this, but intervening could set that killer free for good. Makenzie balled her fists, trying to form a plan.

As they passed the window, the man stumbled, and his blue eyes met hers through the glass.

Blue eyes.

Familiar eyes.

Ian Andrews's eyes.

Makenzie Fuller? What was she doing here?

Ian Andrews stumbled and shook his head, trying to clear it.

Had he been drinking?

No, he didn't drink. Did he? Not in… Not in years.

He'd been sipping orange-and-cranberry juice when the newcomer had bumped into him, hitting his drink hand. Obscuring it for a moment.

Wait. He'd been drugged.

He stumbled again, and the man he was with chuckled and jerked him to his feet.

It didn't sound like a friendly chuckle.

But it did sound incredibly far away.

Lifting his hand, Ian stared at his fingers. Or were they his? They seemed disconnected, as though they belonged to someone else's body. Maybe they belonged to the man he was walking with?

Where were they anyway? He lifted his head and tried to prop his chin on the man's shoulder, to get a look at his surroundings. How had he gotten here? He was meeting someone. There was something about the weather…a storm.

Alarms in his head said he should run.

He couldn't. His feet barely kept pace

with the guy helping him across the uneven ground.

He was tired. So tired.

With every second, he felt more of himself fall away. More creeping darkness ate the edges of his thoughts. "Where—" He lacked the energy to say more. It took all he had not to pitch to the patio under his feet.

"To my car." They passed between an opening in the wall and made their way slowly along a walkway lined on one side by rough stone arches and on the other by a stone wall. "And then?" That dark chuckle came again, sending a shiver down Ian's spine. "Then I'm going to dance with my niece at her wedding."

This was a wedding?

"Butler!" A woman's voice echoed off of the walls and floated past Ian's ears, drifting through the arches into the cold mountain night.

At least he thought he was in the mountains. Maybe only darkness existed. Only this walkway.

Cursing beneath his breath, the man beside him stopped. He stood straighter, and Ian's head slid from his shoulder, his chin dropping to his chest.

His whole body was heavy, his muscles loose. The floor. If he could just lie down on the floor...

"I told you to keep an eye on my niece." His companion's words were angry. "That was an order."

"You're about two seconds from getting caught." The tone of the woman's voice was equally harsh.

Familiar?

Peace washed over him. It started in his chest and flowed like warm syrup all the way to his toes. He could sink into that voice.

He could trust that voice.

Footsteps echoed. Shoes appeared. Expensive black boots with chunky low heels. "Let me handle it. No one will miss me." The shoes stepped closer and the voice dropped. "If anyone sees you, they'll wonder why you're dragging an incapacitated victim away. With me? They'll think he's had too much to drink and he's leaving with a woman. Think about it."

Had he had too much to drink? Was he leaving with this woman? This woman whose voice dropped farther away by the moment, even though she hadn't moved. He slipped lower.

"I gave you an order." The man's grip on Ian tightened and his voice dipped to a growl. "It's possible Nicholson was right about you."

The black boots disappeared. "He's a troublemaker, and you know it." The woman was angry. He didn't know how he knew, but he'd heard that tone before.

This dude had better back off, because she could hurt him.

He tried to lift his head to decipher if she was friend or foe, but his body and mind were disconnected. The stones at his feet wavered. Maybe he was going to be sick.

"Fine. I'll be inside." Footsteps receded, echoing everywhere, even against his skull.

"Let's get this over with." The man jerked Ian upright, practically dragging him the last few feet to a car that waited with the door open.

Ian's head cracked the frame as the man shoved him into the passenger seat then slammed the door.

The pain jarred his thoughts. For an instant, clarity returned.

He'd been drugged. This was a kidnapping.

If he was judging the situation correctly, it was about to be a murder.

He reached for the door handle and missed. The world existed in a tunnel.

The car rocked as the man climbed into the driver's seat and slammed the door, then reached over and buckled Ian's seat belt, muttering. "Last thing I need is to get pulled over." He shoved Ian roughly toward the door. "I've got a celebration to attend."

Ian's head banged against the window as the car accelerated and started down a winding road, deeper into darkness.

He had to stop this vehicle if he wanted to survive.

With the last of his consciousness slipping away, he focused on one set of muscles. One action.

Lurching to the side, he grabbed the steering wheel and jerked it downward.

A sickening swerve.

Skidding tires.

Cracking trees.

The world disappeared.

TWO

No.

Makenzie slammed on the brakes. The rear of her high-end SUV fishtailed before it stopped.

She clenched her jaw. Butler's car had skidded, nearly corrected, then disappeared off a curve, ripping through trees and down an embankment.

Ian was in that car. No matter what the government accused him of, he didn't deserve to die.

Pressing the gas pedal to the floor, she roared toward the curve and stopped again, jumping out of the vehicle while it still rocked from the sudden stop. She shoved her phone into her pocket and made sure her pistol was secure in the holster at her ribs, then ran around the car to the edge of the road.

The land dropped off suddenly, plunging about thirty feet to a broad, shallow riverbed.

Butler's BMW rested in the water, a dark silhouette in the starlight.

Activating the flashlight on her phone, Makenzie scanned the ground and picked out a way down. Two steps in, the bigger problem emerged.

The overskirt to her pantsuit snagged every bush and limb.

She hated this op. Hated the outfit.

At least she'd worn boots. Thin, dressy boots, but still boots.

Shoving her phone in her pocket, she grabbed the sides of the black overskirt and ripped it away. The white pants beneath glowed in the starlight. So much for concealment.

Makenzie moved as quickly as she dared.

Maybe she could still save her cover. Tell Butler and his minions she'd followed him to protect him.

If anyone in the car was still alive.

At the bottom of the ravine, her feet hit water. It was only seconds before icy cold invaded her thin boots. She waded in knee-deep, the sluggish current of the shallow river tugging at her wide-legged pants, numbing her calves and pulling her off-balance.

The car rested on its wheels in the water. The driver's side roof had smashed against the boulder that had abruptly ended its descent.

Through the fractured windshield, the condition of Robert Butler's body left no doubt the crushing blow to the roof had ended his life.

Makenzie gulped down nausea, her body convulsing with shock and cold. He was a criminal, a killer, but this was horrid.

Taking several bracing breaths of chilled mountain air, she steadied herself. She needed to check on Ian.

Please, Lord. I've already lost one partner.

Although Ian had ceased to be her partner the day he disappeared.

Still… *Don't let him be dead.* If he was, her heart would break for the second time since his betrayal. He'd be irrevocably gone…and he'd be unable to face justice if the accusations against him were true.

She prayed every day they were a colossal misunderstanding.

Limbs numbing in the icy water, Makenzie fought her way around the car, preparing herself for the worst.

The damage to the passenger side was negligible. Shining her light into the shattered window, she found Ian slumped over the seat belt.

Makenzie reached into the car. Her frozen fingers found his neck.

His pulse pumped, steady but slow.

He needed help. Quickly.

She scanned his face and neck for injuries, but none were obvious. He was unconscious, likely from Butler's drug cocktail. The man blended his own mixture, meant to incapacitate from the brain out.

He hadn't killed anyone on Makenzie's

watch, so she had no way of knowing if the drugs themselves were deadly.

She needed to move fast. If Ian—

A bullet sparked against the roof. A gunshot cracked the stillness.

Diving below door level, Makenzie drew her pistol from her chest holster and scanned the road above.

In the blink of her SUV's hazard lights, two figures moved.

Likely some of Butler's men, possibly Cale Nicholson.

If he'd spotted her, then her cover was definitely blown.

Another shot rang off the rocks. She narrowed her eyes. Either they were awful shots or they hadn't seen her and were gunning for the vehicle.

For Butler? Or Ian?

The windshield was already trashed by the wreck. One direct hit could shatter it and leave Ian exposed.

Moving him could paralyze or kill him if he had a neck injury.

Not moving him would sign his death

warrant if the shooters made their way down before she dragged him to safety.

What these guys needed was an audience.

Dimming her phone's screen, Makenzie dialed 911. When the operator answered, she gave her location. "A car went off the road into the river. Somebody's shooting at it. Please hurry." She tried to sound frantic. Even in this situation, she had to maintain cover as long as possible.

Another shot punctuated her plea.

"Ma'am, please stay on—"

"They're coming. I have to go. Just hurry." She killed the call and shoved the phone into the top of her pantsuit, then holstered her pistol. No telling how long it would take help to arrive.

The shooting had stopped.

She scanned the ledge. Nothing moved around her car. They must be picking their way down.

She was out of time. Given the odds were two to one? A shootout would prove deadly.

Reaching through the window, she eased Ian away from the door, praying the metal hadn't been jammed. It opened with a jerk that nearly sprawled her into the river. Shivers worked their way up from her freezing legs.

There were more dangers at play than she'd considered. If they didn't get out of the frigid water, bullets would be the least of their worries.

She surveyed Ian. He was going to be deadweight.

Crouching in the painfully cold water, she shifted him and slung him over her shoulders in a fireman's carry. Grateful for the moonless night, she slogged in the river toward her shooters. They'd expect her to head away. Hopefully, it was dark enough to mask her movements and identity, though her white pantsuit could be a dead giveaway.

Literally.

That was a concern for after they were safe. Dying in a shootout would make a blown cover irrelevant.

Two quick shots skipped the water only a few feet away. Either they were firing blind, or her ridiculous white clothes really did glow.

Stumbling, she doubled back and headed for the rocks on the river's edge. If they could see her, then her only option was to take cover and shoot this out.

There were fifteen bullets in her clip. No backup weapon. No spare ammo.

Fifteen chances to save both of their lives.

Ian groaned but didn't stir. Scanning the low bank, she made out a grouping of rocks tall enough to shield them. *Lord, let it be enough.*

After sliding Ian to the ground in the shelter of a boulder, she rolled him onto his side.

Ducking behind the rock, Makenzie crouched and drew her weapon, searching for motion along the ravine. In the starlight, dim figures inched toward the river, only visible if she didn't look directly at them. No lights. Either they hadn't considered their phones, or they were hoping for concealment.

She gripped the pistol tighter. A fight to

the death wasn't something she relished. *God, if there's another way...*

There probably wasn't. To get Ian and herself out alive, someone else might have to die.

Taking her stance, she steeled herself for battle.

The darkness shifted.

In the distance, an indistinct wail took shape. Multiple wails in multiple tones.

Sirens.

Police. Fire. Ambulance.

Help was close.

Shouts and curses rained from above.

Makenzie wanted to cheer but kept herself in battle position. Yep, the cavalry was coming, but those men still had a choice.

Run and save themselves...

Or finish the job they'd started.

Makenzie prayed.

The shadowy figures reversed course and returned to the top of the cliff. Tires squealed and headlights flashed as a vehicle accelerated away, headed down the mountain.

Slumping forward, Makenzie rested her forehead against the rough rock, her body shuddering with the frigid cold and the drop in adrenaline.

If her cover truly had been blown, their safety would only last until Butler's men could hunt her down to exact their revenge.

Someone was taking a jackhammer to his skull.

Ian winced and lifted his hand, trying to press it against his head. Maybe pressure would stop the thumping pain.

His hand was heavy. Tangled with something that shouldn't be there.

Easing his eyelids open, he tried to see his surroundings, because this definitely wasn't his bed in his apartment in Maryland.

The sickly scent of cafeteria food and antiseptic wafted past. The view of the world that squeezed between his half-closed eyes was a dim beige blur. The light was dim, but the noise... Distant voices. Footsteps. A repeated low click that he couldn't place.

As quiet as it was, it was still too loud for his pounding brain to handle.

He squeezed his eyes shut. "Make that stop." It didn't matter that he'd barked like a drill sergeant. If that click stopped, his brain might sort out what was happening.

"So you're awake?" A woman's voice, vaguely familiar, came from his left. After a slight rustle, the light on the other side of his eyelids grew dimmer. "Because I have so many questions."

"About what?" The words fired like bullets. Her tone was unnecessarily accusatory, and the pain in his head coupled with his confusion stripped away any patience he might normally display.

When he managed to ease his eyes open, a face hovered over his own.

His head pressed into the pillow at the shock, but those few inches of distance made the world fall into focus. Multiple eyes merged until there were only two. One nose. One mouth. Dark brown hair that needed a comb.

Hang on. He knew this woman.

"Makenzie?" Why was she here? Where exactly was here?

A stab of panic rushed through him, and he sat up, narrowly avoiding a collision with the investigator who had joined his team only a week before.

She moved just in time.

The room wobbled. Ian's stomach swooped with the whirls in his vision.

Oh, boy.

Three deep inhales quelled the nausea before it escalated. Gradually, the world stopped rolling.

A curtained wall. Monitors. Wires and tubes.

A hospital?

He sank against the pillows before the room could pitch again and turned his head gently to the woman who stood beside the bed, arms crossed over her chest. A scowl marred her otherwise attractive face.

Makenzie Fuller had arrived in Maryland a week earlier. Her partner had been murdered, and she'd been reassigned from the team that Eagle Overwatch fielded near

Portland. There was something else about her...

Whatever it was disappeared in the fog.

Why was she here? Where was his partner, Gage? "What happened?"

Her expression softened, as though the question cracked her unexplained anger. She settled on a chair beside his bed and sat back, crossing her arms over her stomach as though she could hold herself together. "You were in a car accident."

"A what?" *No way.* He couldn't even remember being in a car. The last thing he remembered was...

Was...

Nothing. The past was fuzzy. Nebulous. Like trying to see the Milky Way in the night sky. If he focused too hard, the whole thing disappeared.

He tried to sit up, but a seasick sway pinned him to the pillow. "Gage. My partner. You remember him, right? Is he okay?" Because the only reason his partner wouldn't be here was if the accident Ian couldn't remember had taken Gage's life. The thought made him almost as sick as whatever was barnstorming inside his skull.

"Gage Ortiz?" Makenzie dropped her hands to her lap and leaned closer. The confusion on her face was clear. There seemed to be doubt, too. "You're asking about Special Agent Gage Ortiz?"

Why was this so hard for her to understand? "Yes. My partner. Dark hair. Scar on his forehead. We've chatted with you a couple of times. You made fun of his Yankees shirt. Told him you were a Red Sox fan."

"I mean, yeah, that happened." The words were drawn out. Then she shook her head, eyebrows knitting together over impressive green eyes. "Your partner?" She tilted her head. "What do you mean by *we've chatted with you a couple of times*?"

This woman talked in riddles. Either that or his brain was scrambled. Ian tried again to sit up, but the motion was too much. He wanted to grab her hand and make her spill whatever she withheld. "This. Just tell me Gage is okay." He was supposed to have his partner's back. He couldn't do that if he had no idea where Gage was.

"He's—" Her hand waved toward the curtain. "You know as much as I do about Gage."

Actually, he didn't. "Is he alive?" Ian said the words slowly. Maybe they'd break through this woman's mental block if he enunciated.

"Last time I heard." Her tight posture screamed a warning Ian couldn't decipher. She leaned closer and her gaze turned to ice. "Are you saying you spent time with Gage recently?"

"Are you saying I didn't?" He couldn't remember when. He had a thousand memories of his partner. They'd just finished investigating a company commander for identity theft. The case dragged on for months and they'd often crammed in fast food long after everyone else in the world had hit the rack. They'd returned to Maryland last week.

He couldn't grab on to one of those memories of Gage and call it *the last time*. Vague panic worked its way up from his stomach. Something was wrong, but not with Gage.

With him.

Makenzie stared at him hard. She was definitely angry.

Beneath the anger, it almost looked as though his words caused her pain.

"Ian, this is a really sick game. I didn't want to believe it was true." She turned her face to the ceiling, her voice a deadly whisper. "Whatever you're into, it's over. Talk to me. Truthfully."

His eyes widened. First off, she made no sense. Second, she didn't know him well enough to talk to him like this. They might be teammates, but that didn't give her the right to go toe-to-toe—

Toe-to-toe. An image zipped through his mind, winging by like a bat in the darkness. Boots. An argument. He sensed it more than saw it, but the impression it left was a deep-seated certainty that he should be afraid for his life.

His hand searched until his fingers brushed the bed's controls and raised him higher.

He needed to run far away from Makenzie Fuller, because his problems started with her.

Had she gone rogue?

He scanned her from head to waist. She wore a white formal pants thing that had seen better days. Her shoulders were wrapped in a blanket that matched the one on his bed. "Were you in the accident, too?" He balled his fists. Why couldn't he remember?

"Oh, come *on*." With a frustrated sigh, she rocketed from the chair, dragging the blanket with her. "It's me. Tell the truth." She bit off the words as though they tasted bitter.

"What truth?" If he thought he could manage without falling, he'd stand and confront her. Call their team leader and demand an explanation.

But even sitting up in bed had his vision going all Tilt-A-Whirl.

As suddenly as her temper flared, Makenzie deflated. She was like a little girl wrapped in her security blanket.

He almost wanted to hug her.

Fixing her eyes on the foot of his bed, she shook her head as though regret weighed her low. "You really did it, didn't you?"

"I really did what?" He exhaled his frustration. "Why won't you give me a straight answer?"

Throwing her hands into the air as though she'd like to take a swing at him, Makenzie whipped around and parted the curtain, disappearing through it.

Her absence made him feel lonely and… guilty?

An overwhelming tide of guilt swamped him. Beneath it, nagging concern swelled into fear.

There'd been an accident he couldn't remember.

His heart picked up the pace as he dug through the fog. Yesterday he'd had a bagel for breakfast and had met Gage to wrap up a landslide of paperwork about their investigation.

Today?

Somewhere up the hallway, alarm bells pinged. A nurse rushed into the room.

Makenzie followed.

For all of her anger and cryptic comments, he was almost happy to see her. At least he knew who she was.

She stood by the curtain, wrapped in her blanket, holding his gaze as the nurse silenced his monitor and looked down at him. "Mr. Andrews." Her smile was too broad. "It's good to see you awake. Can I ask you some questions?"

He tore his gaze from the green eyes across the room. A thousand questions sat on his tongue, but he didn't know how to ask them. "Sure."

"What's your name?"

"Ian Michael Andrews."

"Do you know where you are?"

"The hospital." He flicked a quick glance at Makenzie. "I don't know which one."

The nurse nodded. "Greenville Memorial."

"North Carolina?" Why was he hours away from home?

"Actually you're in Greenville, *South* Carolina." The nurse's smile etched into place. "Where do you think you should be?"

"Maryland."

Makenzie shifted. Her face flickered with surprise. Once again, wounded anger burned beneath the surface.

He'd said something wrong.

"Ian, what day is it?" The nurse laid a hand on his wrist, checking his pulse.

He rattled off the date and the president's name. He knew how this worked. He'd seen hospital TV shows.

The nurse's grip tightened. The smile slipped. Patting him on the arm, she checked his monitor. "I'll tell Dr. Eviston you're awake. She'll want to chat."

The nurse disappeared through the curtain with a pointed look at Makenzie.

Makenzie turned from watching the nurse leave. "Ian, stop the charade. I know you well enough to know what you're trying to pull."

This woman needed to back off. "You met me last week. We are not friends."

Her head jerked as though he'd slapped her. Tears crowded the corners of her eyes. "I can't believe you'd do this."

Whoa. She might be confusing him, but he hadn't meant to hurt her. "Look, Makenzie, I—"

She held up her hand and pierced him with an icy gaze. "I don't know why you're pretending you don't know me. If you think it's going to keep you out of prison, you're wrong. If everything they say about you is true, then nothing can save you."

THREE

The instant her words landed, Makenzie wished she could take them back.

Ian's face literally drained of color. "What are you talking about?" His tone was defiant, a mismatch to his obvious shock.

Makenzie's heart tangled with the memory of the trust they'd shared in their partnership... Trust that had once grown into so much more.

What if he wasn't faking his condition?

Even so, he couldn't explain his disappearing act immediately before a new hacker started offering his services to the worst of humanity. Immediately after they'd talked about—

Balling her fists, she exhaled the past away. Too much was at stake. Too many questions needed answers.

The first involved what he was doing at the wedding of a known arms dealer's niece. An arms dealer who wanted him dead for double-crossing an *associate*. An arms dealer who was now dead.

She'd have to call her team leader to debrief. Should have done it already, but concern for Ian had derailed her tactical mind.

"Seriously." Ian sat up, his heart monitor spiking as he wobbled with the change in position. "What do you think—"

"I hear Mr. Andrews is awake." A woman breezed in, all business yet wearing a friendly smile. Her brown hair bobbed in a ponytail, gray streaking through it like tinsel. She stopped by Makenzie as the nurse slipped in behind her. "I'm Dr. Eviston. Would you mind stepping out while I examine Mr. Andrews?"

Makenzie started to protest, then merely nodded. While undercover, she carried no credentials. She wasn't Ian's family. Visiting hours were long over. If she raised a fuss, they could start asking questions she couldn't answer. They'd escort her out; then what would she have?

A dead arms dealer, a blown cover and a questionable former partner.

She really needed to call her team leader.

With a last glance at Ian, she slipped into the hallway and headed for a small alcove. It provided the perfect spot to speak privately where no one could sneak up on her. This late at night, the ICU was relatively quiet but, in her job, she could never be too careful.

Her overworked boots slipped on the polished floor. If she wasn't undercover, she'd have had a change of clothes in her car. As it was, she was stuck in her water-stained pantsuit and thin-soled leather dress boots. At least in a hospital, no one had looked twice at her disheveled appearance.

In the alcove, she dropped onto the edge of a chair and dialed the number.

"Fuller, what are you doing? You aren't supposed to reach out to me, only to your handler." Major Jayla Tangaro answered on the first ring, almost as though she'd been

waiting for Makenzie's call. "Is the op compromised?"

*I'm safe, Major. Thanks for your con-
cern.* Makenzie bit her tongue. Tangaro
was a no-nonsense team leader who had
been business-first since the day Makenzie transferred to Maryland after her former partner Audra's murder in Tacoma four
years earlier.

There were multiple teams scattered
around the world as part of Eagle Overwatch, a top-secret unit that ran deep cover
operations for the army. They investigated
the investigators or went undercover in sit-
uations where it was believed corruption
reached the highest levels.

While the major was concerned for the
safety of all her subordinates, she wasn't
necessarily vocal about it.

"Fuller?" Major Tangaro's tone shifted.
"What's going on?"

"I'm not sure." Best to be up-front. Tangaro wasn't a fan of dragging things out.

She skipped Ian's presence to focus on
her mission, giving a quick rundown of

Butler's death and the unknown assailants at the crash scene. "Whether I've had my cover blown or not, Nicholson has been squawking about my position in the organization. Given that Butler's dead and I've vanished after he gave orders for me to stay put? They're going to trust me less than they already do. I'll guarantee there's already a plan to take me out."

Tangaro muttered under her breath.

Makenzie probably didn't want to decipher it. This op had been ongoing for a year, and it had been plagued by disaster from two days before it started.

The day that Ian had vanished, leaving her to go in alone, without her partner.

She'd managed well until today, when he'd mysteriously reappeared.

Makenzie massaged her temple. She'd gathered so much evidence... If she'd been outed as an undercover agent, the group would either scatter with Butler's death or would close up ranks and go underground to regroup. She'd be shut out.

"Okay, Fuller. We may be able to work

with this. We can make a raid in the power vacuum left behind with his death. We'll sweep up who's left and see if any of them talk about who's working on the inside to get those weapons off those bases."

"I think there's an opportunity to scoop up an even bigger fish."

"Who?"

"Someone going by the code name Storm."

Tangaro snorted. "That's original."

"Original or not, Butler was awfully excited about a meeting with them. Kept talking about going international."

"There's no Storm on our radar. No pun intended. You're sure?"

"Someone delivered a second laptop to Butler three days ago. He's been buzzing about this meeting for days. I'm sure."

A tapping sound came through the line, like a pen against a notepad. "Can you reach out? Who trusted you on Butler's crew? See if they're truly against you."

"Butler trusted me. The men were pretty hostile." They'd been jealous. She'd heard the not-so-quiet whispers about how she obtained her position. All lies, of course, but the men preferred soothing their egos over telling the truth. She'd fought small power battles every single day, struggling to hold on to her authority.

One possibility stood out. "I can contact Kevin Glazer. He wasn't more fond of me than the rest, but he's a terrible liar. If they're onto me, he won't be able to cover." She'd claim she was following Butler to protect him and had gone into hiding after the shooting, assuming that whoever was pulling the trigger was after her as well.

It could be a deadly risk to take.

"Do that. Maintain your cover as long as possible, which means don't risk reaching out unless you need extraction or you're prepared to shut this down. Butler might be gone, but we still need access to who is helping him on those bases. That's our main focus. If we can get this Storm as well? Gather all you can. Then—"

"Wait." Makenzie took a deep breath and held it. No one interrupted Major Tangaro without a serious verbal beating. The major had endured her own power struggles as she rose through the ranks to lead her own team of undercover operatives.

Right now wasn't the time to worry about that. She still had Ian on her hands. Overwatch would want him ASAP. "There's one more thing you need to be aware of."

"More?"

"Special Agent Ian Andrews."

"What about him?" The major's tone sharpened. No one on the team was a fan of Ian's. He'd definitely been found guilty without a trial and on the basis of circumstantial evidence. The only thing he could truly be pinned with was desertion.

That was bad enough.

"Fuller?" The major was losing her patience.

"He's with me." Makenzie braced for impact.

The tension was so taut it seemed to crackle. "How?"

"He's the man Butler drugged and was—"

"You potentially blew your cover for

Ian Andrews?" The anger was real and viciously hot. "You should have let—"

"Major Fuller." This time Makenzie didn't care if she got reamed. The major didn't need to regret an emotional outburst like the one she was about to have. "If he's guilty of hacking for the bad guys, he'll face justice. If he's not, he'll be vindicated."

The major sighed, the sound alarmingly human. "What does he have to say for himself?"

Ian had been a friend to them all, a trusted teammate. When it became clear his disappearance wasn't foul play, they'd all been wounded.

No one had felt the cut more than Makenzie.

Given his current state of either brain-rattling or treachery, she wasn't sure she wanted to report anything he'd said. "He was unconscious when they brought him to the hospital. Either the drug or a whack to his head during the accident did some damage."

"We can't risk sending agents down now.

It could point the finger straight at you if anyone is watching."

That was true. "So he's in my custody?" How would she juggle her undercover persona and a wanted man?

"Stick with the initial plan until it's safe to hand him over. You have the safe house at your disposal if necessary."

The safe house. There were comfy, dry clothes there. It was so tempting to trade in the entire op for a hot shower and yoga pants. "Understood."

"Makenzie?"

The major's use of her given name lifted her head. "Yes?"

"Ian Andrews isn't Audra Robinson."

Makenzie winced, the name a blow to her chest.

No one was Audra. What had happened to her was—

She shivered and willed the images from her mind. No human being deserved what had happened to Audra.

Least of all Audra. A top-notch investigator. A patient partner during Makenzie's training. An investigative ninja.

She sniffed and stood. "Nobody needs to remind me of that."

"Even Audra wasn't Audra, at least not the way you remember her." The major almost sounded like a parent. "Someday you'll have to take her off that pedestal you've set her on."

Opening her mouth to argue, Makenzie thought better of it. She'd been accused more than once of idolizing her first partner, but no one had known her the way Makenzie had. Her goal in life was to be the kind of investigator Audra had been. Fair and thorough.

Killing the call before she could be deemed insubordinate, she eyed the entrance to Ian's room with her lips twisted.

She'd have to remain vigilant. More vigilant than she'd been when they suspected someone was stalking Audra. Ian was now her responsibility. She'd lost one partner, and she wouldn't lose another.

Not even one who'd vanished under questionable circumstances, crushing her in a way no one else ever could.

Whether Ian was truly injured or was working a scheme to protect his future, one thing was clear from the evening's events. Someone wanted him dead, and she was the only person who could protect him.

Retrograde amnesia.

The words the doctor had patiently repeated tumbled in Ian's head. *Blood tests. Drug cocktail. Police have questions.*

The only word that made sense was *amnesia.*

People only got that in movies, right?

Apparently not.

Ian stared at the drop ceiling and let his eyes shift out of focus, blurring the straight lines between ceiling panels. "My name is Ian Michael Andrews." He'd said it repeatedly. Along with his birthday, his home address and the date his parents had been killed in a small plane crash.

Everything else was mush. In his mind,

Gage was his partner and they'd just completed a mission in Texas.

In reality, he'd lost four years.

Panic shot through him. Where was Makenzie? She seemed to know him better than she should. Maybe she did. In his four-year memory gap, they could have become the best of friends.

Could she fill in the blanks?

Or was she the one who'd injected him with the drug that had robbed him of his present-day self?

There was one way to find out if she was telling the truth. Grabbing the phone, he dialed Gage's number.

Three tones. "We're sorry, the number you have dialed has been disconnected or is no longer—"

He slammed the phone into the cradle like it was on fire. Makenzie might be telling the truth.

Nausea crashed into his stomach, too strong to be eradicated by the medication the nurse had given him. He wanted to curl into the fetal position until it passed, but that wasn't his style.

He might not remember last Christmas, but he knew the kind of man he was, and he could take down whoever had done this to him.

Just reminding himself of that made his head feel clearer.

Okay, he'd call Major Tangaro. His team leader would—

Someone cleared their throat.

Makenzie stood at the curtain, eyeing him with a look both suspicious and sad. Apparently, someone had taken pity on her battered outfit and handed over a set of scrubs. The loose black clothing made her look like a ninja.

When he'd met her for the first time, he'd thought she was more than passably attractive with dark hair that waved to her shoulders and green eyes that were impossibly clear. Now, with her face freshly scrubbed and her hair in disarray, she was even more striking.

She was also more confusing than anything else in his upside-down world. "What are we to each other?"

She twitched as though a bullet had slammed into her. "What?"

Clearly, that wasn't the question she'd expected.

"In the four years I don't remember, we obviously stayed on the same team. What's our relationship?" The words came out with more authority than he'd intended, but he was desperate for familiarity in a reality he didn't recognize. It felt as though he'd walked into a movie during the climax, clueless about how the story had reached this point.

"That's a discussion for later." She strode across the room with authority of her own and stood a few feet from his bed. "You have amnesia?"

"So they tell me."

"I'm not sure I buy it."

Interesting. He found the button and eased the bed higher, unwilling to look up at her from a vulnerable position.

He needed answers, not more tap-dancing. "You know me, but you don't trust me." He scratched his cheek. "Did I lie to you?" He didn't believe he was capable of cruelty, but strange things could have happened to him he couldn't remember. "Did we date and I cheated on you?"

She froze. A long beat passed, then she laughed too loudly. "You never had the opportunity."

So they hadn't dated. Odd, because she almost acted like a jilted ex.

"You said I've been accused of something. I deserve to know what that is." The antinausea drug had made him drowsy, but it helped with the wooziness that clouded his thinking. He was feeling more like himself...whoever that was.

He wanted answers.

"We're both investigators." She approached and rested her hands on the bed rail.

"This much I know."

"As an investigator, you know not to feed a person too much information. You want to see what they'll tell you on their own. Well, I need to know if what you're saying is true. You have no head injury. I heard the doc tell you that. Whatever this is…" She waved her palm in a circle over him. "It's drug induced. No way to really prove it. So I want to see what you have to say before I answer any questions."

Fair enough. As much as he was antsy to know what was happening, he was tired of putting pieces together. "Am I in custody?"

"You're in my—" Raised voices filtered in from the hall. Makenzie's head jerked in that direction, and her expression shifted to concern.

She strode to the curtain and peeked out. The way she stood, hand hovering near her waist, it was obvious she was armed.

Was it to protect him? Or to protect herself *from* him? "What's wrong?"

Without looking back, she held up a hand to silence him.

If only he dared to get out of bed and look for himself. Being tethered to cords and wires while the world passed by was the most helpless he'd ever felt.

More voices, tinged in anger now. After a moment, they faded up the hall.

Makenzie kept watching. Without a word, she disappeared through the curtain.

Whatever was happening involved him. He was busting out of this bed and getting answers. Reaching for his hand, he grasped the IV line, prepared to pull it free.

"Stop." Makenzie rushed into the room. "You'll hurt yourself. Not to mention make a gigantic mess."

She dropped her phone and drove her bootheel into the screen, then kicked it under the bed.

So they were running.

With sure motions, she unhooked Ian from the wires and tubes that held him prisoner. Guess she'd excelled in the field-medicine portion of basic training. "We have to get out of here."

"Why?" He was still slightly suspicious. If this was drug induced, someone had dosed him. He had no proof it wasn't her. Although his gut said she was safe, he wasn't ready to embrace that idea.

"Some guys showed up looking for you, likely to finish what they already started."

"So my car accident wasn't an accident?"

"No." Alarms sounded as she detached the last of the wires. "They're claiming to work for Overwatch. The nurse took them to hospital Security for clearance. In about ten minutes, they'll be back."

If they were assassins, they'd return in *less* than ten minutes.

The young nurse from earlier rushed into the room. "What's going on in here?"

Makenzie whirled to look at Ian, sending silent messages with her gaze.

He had a choice. Did he trust her or not?

His gut said to go with her. "I'm leaving. I don't want to be here, and you can't keep me."

Ian swung his legs over the side of the bed. It took every aching muscle in his banged up body not to wobble. Antinausea meds did a lot, but they didn't fully reset equilibrium, that was for sure.

"Whoa." The nurse was at his side, one hand on his shoulder and the other on his back. "You can't leave. Dr. Eviston hasn't—"

"You think those men outside are federal agents and he's a fugitive, right?" Makenzie stared down the nurse, who paled and refused to meet anyone's eyes. "They're lying. They aren't agents. They're involved with the man who drugged Mr. Andrews. If they return and he's here, they'll kill him."

The nurse's hold on him slackened and she backed away a step. "I don't believe—"

"Believe it." Ian spoke with more authority than he felt and moved to stand, then he glanced down. This backless hospital gown wasn't going to cut it. "Scrubs?" He gave her a hopeful look.

Hard to tell if the nurse was angry or scared. She exhaled loudly and made a wide berth around Makenzie as she left the room.

They were asking too much of her, but this was an emergent situation. No way was he running around with nothing but a gown between him and the outside world. Bare legs weren't going to do it.

"I can't believe you're holding us up for clothes." Makenzie muttered. "We need to move and, the way you're wobbling, we won't be doing that quickly."

He shot her a withering look.

She sighed. "You've got ten seconds—"

Like an answered prayer, the nurse blew in and dropped a pair of sweats and a tee on the bed. They were huge, made for a Heisman Trophy winner.

Ian didn't care.

With an exasperated sigh, Makenzie stepped out of the room behind the nurse. "Five seconds."

He could hear her talking outside, mapping an exit strategy with the reluctant nurse. Holding the pants at the waist, Ian worked his way to the hall, rocking slightly, praying he didn't topple over. "Let's bounce."

Looking him up and down, Makenzie smirked. "Between your mixed-up head and those pants just begging to trip you, we might." Offering him her arm for support, she headed up the hall to the elevator, pausing at the nurse's station. "Call the police. Tell them you have two men in the hospital impersonating federal agents. Do not tell anyone you saw us."

The handful of nurses clustered in the station watched as they passed. One chewed her lower lip.

Ian gripped Makenzie's arm and wished he didn't have to lean on her. He wasn't feeble. He was ready to fight.

Except the fog in his thinking said he wasn't. Every step was a nightmare of brain-jarring, floor-tilting proportions. Flight was not the best idea in his condition, but he had a feeling if he wanted to live past the next five minutes, it was the only option.

Once they were in the main hall, he tried to plan and be of some use. "Okay, Mac-Gyver. You get us out of the building, then what? You called a rideshare?"

"I followed the ambulance here in my car." She stopped to peek around the corner.

"You drove your own vehicle? Aren't you worried about GPS tracking?"

"You really don't remember me, do you?" At another set of swinging doors, she shot him an annoyed glance. "I disabled it a long time ago. There's a signal blocker to handle any attempted add-ons."

He shook his head as she peeked through the door.

Shouts echoed. Footsteps thudded.

Makenzie ducked and shot him a worried glance. "Ian, it's time to run."

FOUR

Makenzie shoved Ian back down the hallway.

He stumbled and reached for the wall.

She winced. Whatever Butler had dosed him with, it was doing a number on him.

They couldn't afford to slow down. The hallway offered no protection. She certainly didn't want to engage in a firefight in a hospital.

They probably had fifteen seconds before Nicholson and one of his hangers-on, Phineas Fogarty, reached them.

Ian tugged her arm. "Elevator."

Making their way the few feet to the metal doors felt like it took hours. She punched the button and, in answer to her silent prayers, the door slid open. They stumbled in and the door shut as Butler's men burst through the swinging doors.

Ian punched every button on the panel and leaned heavily against the wall.

Smart thinking. If the elevator stopped at every floor, no one would know which one they'd chosen to exit.

As the doors opened on the second floor, Makenzie and Ian pressed their backs to the wall.

She held her Sig at the ready.

No one waited.

As the door slid closed, she gave herself five seconds to breathe. Fogarty and Nicholson knew she was here, that she was helping Ian escape.

Butler's entire organization would turn on her now.

Which meant they were both on the run.

"Which floor?" Ian should be in a hospital bed detoxing from Butler's attack. It was obvious from the slightly off-centered focus of his gaze that he was not doing well.

She had to get him somewhere safe before he collapsed, but that required moving quickly, which he wasn't capable of. If he pitched to the floor, he could do worse damage.

Still, they had to try. "We'll get off at four, make our way to the next bank of elevators and head down. Hopefully there's only two of them and they're checking every floor. I'm parked in the emergency lot."

"No. That's the first place they'll look." He eyed her as the doors opened on the third floor. "You can disable a GPS, so I'm guessing you can hot-wire an older vehicle?"

He guessed right, but jimmying a door could prove difficult. Metal coat hangers weren't easy to come by. Neither were vehicles that were easy to hot-wire.

First they had to get out of the building.

She catalogued their assets.

She was in scrubs. Sure, she had no hospital ID, but if she could get Ian into a wheelchair, it was unlikely she'd be questioned. They'd move faster and it would block enough of her body to keep it from being obvious she had no credentials.

Stepping out of the elevator on four, she surveilled the area. Two wheelchairs waited in an alcove.

Ian stepped out, following her gaze. "No."

She should have known he'd balk. He'd never liked being perceived as weak. Healthy competition had driven their partnership. "Would you rather be pushed in a wheelchair or be, you know, *dead*?"

He huffed. "Fine." Grumbling, he leaned on her as they headed to the chairs. He seemed relieved to be seated, though he'd never admit it.

Shoving her Sig into the pocket on the back of the chair, she hurriedly pushed Ian around the corner before either of Butler's minions could exit one of the two elevators that were moving up.

She made a series of turns and headed up a hallway, seeking distance over direction for now.

They passed another bank of elevators and turned again. Before Ian had regained consciousness, she'd had time to study the hospital map in a packet in his room. There were several elevators in the interlocking buildings. *Lord, let us find one that Butler's men aren't watching.*

She didn't pray for help stealing a car. That seemed like a definite gray area.

At the next elevator, she stopped and leaned down to Ian. "You ready?"

"I'd be more ready if I was armed, but..." He looked over his shoulder, meeting her gaze. "Let's do this."

Ignoring the fire that his gaze blasted out of her memory, Makenzie straightened. She'd shelved any idea of a relationship with Ian on the day he vanished so thoroughly that even her elite team couldn't find him. There was no going back, not when he'd been well aware how she felt about betrayal and lies.

She punched the elevator button with a little too much force and watched the numbers slowly climb. *Lord, don't let this be the one elevator in the hospital that Nicholson is on. Please.*

If that was the case, they'd be dead in thirty seconds.

The doors opened, and a huge hulk of a man wearing jeans and a button-down shirt stepped forward.

Makenzie's hand went for her weapon, although she didn't recognize him as one of Butler's lackeys. That didn't mean there wasn't hired muscle running around.

The man eyed Makenzie, and his gaze slipped to Ian. He stepped closer.

Her fingers closed around the pistol's grip.

The man peered down the hall, and Ian tensed so much that Makenzie could almost feel it. Any more and he'd rocket out of the chair.

Likely onto his face.

She tried not to wince. This had to be hard for him.

Finally, the hulk offered a tentative smile. "They're moving my mom from ICU. Can you tell me where the step-down unit is for cardiac patients?"

Makenzie kept her hand on her Sig. It could be a ruse. "Down the hall to the right."

"Thank you." He looked relieved. "It's been a long few days." With a quick smile, he hustled past and disappeared around a corner.

"You have no idea." Just in case he re-appeared, Makenzie smiled around the muttered words then rushed Ian onto the elevator. She didn't relax until the doors closed.

Ian twisted around in the chair. "How did you know where CICU was?"

"I read the sign by the elevator." She'd laugh if they were in the clear.

Which they weren't. They still had to get to the parking lot.

And steal a car.

That idea wasn't sitting well with her. Anyone parked nearby would be here be-cause of a crisis. She didn't relish adding to someone's stress and pain.

Running through the map in her head, she calculated where they were in the build-ing and where they'd exit the elevator.

They'd come out on the same side as the emergency room. "I think we should try for my vehicle." She patted the pocket on the scrubs, reassuring herself that she had the key fob.

"No." Ian turned to look up at her. His eyes still had that glassy look that said his brain wasn't all the way online.

"I don't have time to disable another GPS tracker. Even if I find a car to hot-wire, it could be traced to the safe house. Then we'll have local law enforcement to deal with. There will be a BOLO." She watched the panel tick down to the first floor. "We need to take our chances."

"I don't—"

"Besides." The doors slid open and she glanced out. The only person in the hallway was a nurse walking away from them. "I won't look suspicious coming out of the ER with you in this chair. It's faster than we were moving earlier."

Even from behind, she could tell his jaw hardened. Yeah, she wouldn't like to be the helpless one either.

She rushed up the hall toward the ER. They should be safe there. Even in the middle of the night, it would be packed with the sick and injured. Butler's men wouldn't bring attention to themselves by opening fire around witnesses. Their money was made in the shadows. They wouldn't risk themselves by making a scene in public.

There were no guarantees once she wheeled Ian outside the safety of hospital walls.

The worst was yet to come.

At the double doors to the waiting room, she stopped. "We're going straight through. You know the drill. Act like we belong and everyone will believe we belong." She squared her shoulders and prepared to look the part. "We'll book it when we hit the parking lot."

"You can't push this chair and wield a gun at the same time." Ian held his hand up, waiting.

He wanted her weapon. If he was still her partner... If he hadn't disappeared... If she could truly believe he hadn't turned traitor to team and country...

He might be in danger, but she wasn't

certain which side he was playing on. She'd been burned in the past by people who were supposed to be looking out for her, people she'd trusted.

All she knew for certain was someone wanted Ian dead, and it was her job to protect him.

Makenzie ignored his request and punched the button that swung open the doors.

Pushing through, she fixed on the sliding doors that led to the parking lot.

To freedom or to death.

No one seemed to pay them any mind as they swept out the doors and into the night.

Ian's head was on a swivel, scanning the area. "Where's the car?" The way he gripped the arms of the chair said the motion wasn't helping his equilibrium.

"To the left. Two rows back. A silver BMW SUV."

"Nice."

"It's a company vehicle." The words dripped sarcasm. Butler wanted the criminal world to believe he was some James-

Bond-type villain, and he made sure his people looked the very posh part.

Clear of the door, Makenzie broke into a jog. If anyone questioned why she was hustling across the parking lot pushing a—

"Hey!" The shout came from the right, near the corner of the building. "Nicholson! Found them!"

Makenzie turned toward the shout. Fogarty was on the other side of the parking lot.

She gauged the distance to the car. She was closer to it than Fogarty was to her, but she was also pushing a wheelchair.

Forget pretense. Ripping the key fob from her pocket, she dropped it in Ian's lap. "Unlock the doors."

Out of the corner of her eye, Fogarty stopped running and drew his pistol.

Rookie mistake. It would be hard to hit a moving target. If he was smart, he'd have closed the distance between them.

Good thing he wasn't—

The window beside her shattered. The sound of the shot cracked.

Makenzie ducked. Then again, even not-so-smart could pull off a lucky shot.

A bullet thwacked into the car she was crouched behind as she inched forward.

"Knock it off, Fogarty!" Nicholson's voice was winded. He was somewhere behind them.

Fogarty was to the right.

The car was at the point of a deadly triangle.

One row to go.

She needed to lay down cover fire.

She peered through the windows, making sure no civilians were in sight. Easing up, she fired across the car's trunk, first in Fogarty's direction, then in Nicholson's.

Both men ducked.

She rounded the SUV and threw open the door for Ian, then bolted for the driver's door.

Diving into the driver's side, she started the engine and backed out with tires screeching as onlookers poured from the ER.

Witnesses.

Nicholson and Fogarty stopped, watching helplessly as she sped past them.

When Nicholson's eyes met hers, there was no doubt.

His scowl was a death notice.

As Makenzie backed her car into the garage under the large A-frame house buried in trees on the side of a mountain, Ian let his eyes slip shut. *Thank You, Lord.*

He'd made it out of the hospital and along winding mountain roads for over an hour, and that could only be an answer to prayer. That last climb up a gravel road and a steep, narrow drive had just about done him in.

He'd managed to survive the physical strain and the dizziness without losing whatever his last meal had been. That would have completed his humiliation.

He exhaled through pursed lips as Makenzie shut off the SUV. "Where are we?"

A flicker of sadness ghosted her face in the glow from the headlights. Interesting. It was clear she didn't trust him. Eventually, she'd have to enlighten him as to why…and as to why he brought her pain.

That could wait though. All he wanted now was sleep. He'd been through so much that he wasn't sure he could feel his own body any longer.

"We're at a safe house." Opening the door, Makenzie slipped out and looked over her shoulder at him. "Careful. The wall is close on your side." When she slammed the driver's door, the car rocked. "There's no garage entry under the house. You'll have to walk up the outside stairs."

The slamming door was enough to activate the nausea again. *Great.* His swimming brain took a second to regain equilibrium. As the automatic headlights clicked off, he climbed out of the car and walked out of the garage.

Gingerly.

This was not who he was. The weak one. The cared-for one.

The one who had no idea who his present self was.

Moss-covered steps wound up the side of

the house to a wraparound deck that probably offered incredible views in the daylight. As it was, the starlight revealed only the vague outlines of a thick forest surrounding them and a rising mountain across the road.

Behind him, the garage door rumbled shut.

Gripping the handrail, Ian made his way carefully up the stairs and crossed the porch into the house, closing and locking the door behind him.

Makenzie was nowhere in sight. The room wasn't large, but it was tastefully decorated. An open kitchen held a small island on the other side of the den. A dining table sat to the right. Heavy curtains covered the lower part of the floor-to-ceiling windows that dominated the right wall and climbed into the A-frame.

A leather couch and recliner rested in front of him.

That recliner looked like a gift from heaven. Nothing had ever made him happier.

At least nothing he could remember.

It took the last of his energy to drop into the chair and rest his head against the leather. He didn't even have enough in reserve to raise the footrest. Seated and not moving was enough.

Ian shut his eyes. If he pretended hard enough, he could almost believe he was home in his own recliner.

If he even still owned that chair. Or that condo.

At the moment, he really didn't want to know.

Footsteps came from the short hallway. Ian opened one eye slightly, just to make sure Makenzie wasn't about to shoot him in the head.

The way his brain thudded against the inside of his skull, he might not care if she did.

She didn't spare him a glance. Just veered into the kitchen and opened the refrigerator, mumbling to herself in a way that seemed familiar, though he'd never seen her do that.

Had he?

Preferring the darkness to the puzzles,

he closed his eyes. She might not believe he was stuck in some mental no-man's-land, but he didn't trust her much either. She wasn't exactly forthcoming with information.

For all he knew, she was the one who wanted him dead. Although her taking pot-shots from two goons in a parking lot said that probably wasn't the case.

The light faded, and he peeked to find her standing over him. "Here." She held out a bottle of water.

Thirst slammed him like a body blow. He hadn't realized he was craving fluids until he saw them. Taking the bottle, he then drained half of it before his stomach warned him to slow down. Wiping the back of his hand across his mouth, he tipped the bottle toward her. "Thanks."

Makenzie sank onto the edge of the couch. She'd changed into jeans and an oversize gray sweater with the sleeves pulled over her hands. Her running shoes looked more comfortable than the yellow hospital grip socks he was wearing.

Not fair. "You wouldn't happen to have any me-sized clothes tucked away somewhere, would you?"

She hesitated. Chewed her lower lip. Looked away. "Down the hall. Bedroom on the right."

Ian's eyebrows knit together. "You just happen to have clothes in my size? How do you—" *Wait.* "Are they mine?"

"You keep this innocent act up and I'm going to start believing you." Dropping onto the couch, she slouched with a bottle of water cradled against her stomach.

He needed the truth. To get it, he'd hand her all of the truth he possessed. "Makenzie, listen. I'll level with you."

"Finally."

That raked his last nerve. If he had even half of his head on straight, he'd stand and rain down his frustration until she understood he wasn't lying. He'd always been the guy everyone trusted. Why would this woman who barely knew him treat him this way?

Instead, he counted to ten, then counted

to ten again in Spanish. Started to do it in French but couldn't remember what *four* was. "Let me tell you how I understand my life."

She raised an eyebrow but kept her mouth shut.

"My partner is Gage Ortiz. We've been partners for over two years. I know you from a couple of conversations in the team room. I literally met you a week ago. You came to our team when your partner was killed by an arms dealer who was stalking her."

Makenzie winced.

Clearly, he'd struck another nerve. He'd like to say he was past caring, but her pain struck his heart.

Staring at her water bottle, Makenzie tightened her hold until the plastic popped, then released it. She did it a few more times, the sound echoing off the insides of Ian's skull until he wanted to snatch the thing and hurl it across the room.

Finally, she seemed to notice his discomfort. Sitting forward, she sat the bottle on the glass coffee table. "My partner's name was Audra Robinson."

The name caught on a snag in his memory, then floated away again. He recognized it, but why?

Likely because of Makenzie.

She chewed the inside of her lip, staring at the heavy curtains behind the television. "She was murdered four years ago when we were undercover on an op and her identity was leaked. Her body was burned so badly they had to use dental records to ID her." Snatching the bottle from the table, she stood and walked to the mirror that dominated the wall opposite the A-frame windows.

She stared at him in the reflection. "Your partner Gage left not long after I was transferred to Maryland four years ago. He just…broke. Retired early. Bought a boat and took off for parts unknown."

Gage had talked a little about the scars that came from four brutal deployments. His time as an MP stateside had stretched jagged scars into festering wounds.

He'd also hinted at a future made up of bigger and better things in Overwatch. PTSD could do weird things with the mind though. "I guess I'm not surprised."

"He talked to you about his past?" Makenzie turned and faced him head-on. "Let me guess… He'd been suffering awhile and was afraid of losing his security clearance if he let the pain show?"

It was no secret how many service members tried to hold together lives that were falling to pieces, terrified of losing their jobs if anyone guessed the toll that trauma had taken on them.

He couldn't imagine what would happen once the chain of command at Eagle Overwatch learned he wasn't just traumatized but he had no recollection of the past four years. "So who's my partner now?"

Makenzie's chuckle was quick but bitter. Her lip curled. "Who was your *last* partner, you mean?" With a laugh that might have been more of a sigh, she walked into the kitchen and set her water bottle on the counter. Taking her time, she filled up the carafe for the coffee maker and measured out scoops.

She wouldn't drink it. She didn't like coffee.

Wait. How did he know that?

Unless—"You." That had to be it. It would explain so much about how she was reacting to him. "You're my partner."

"I *was*." She slid the carafe into place and punched the brew button with a little more force than was necessary.

"That's why my clothes are here. We set up this safe house. For an op?"

Makenzie clicked her tongue as she leaned against the island. "For the op I'm on now. Or *was* on."

Carefully, Ian slid to the edge of the chair and planted his feet firmly on the floor, bracing his elbows on his knees. Leaning forward, he stared at the hardwood planks, trying to piece together anything from their past. Flitting bits of emotions wisped by.

He couldn't grasp them.

Still, this explained why she felt familiar. Why, despite the fact he should be concerned she was trying to kill him, inside him rested a deep-seated trust.

What he couldn't puzzle out was the heavy guilt that washed over him at random intervals. The feeling settled in his chest and made it hard to breathe. "What did I do to you?" He addressed the floor, unable to look at her.

"Ian, do you know why you were at that wedding tonight? Why Robert Butler would want you dead so badly that he'd risk taking you out personally?"

Robert Butler. The name conjured a cobblestone in an arched pathway, raising an intense dread.

The image vanished.

The fear didn't.

He tried to ignore it. "I don't know, but I know it's not good." With Makenzie, he got the distinct impression she could sense hesitation and lies.

Honesty was the best way to keep her talking. She held the material to fill in the gaps in his memory. Without her, he had nothing.

She reached for her bottle and gripped it until it popped again. "Butler is an arms dealer. He thought you were a threat to someone close to him, and he was angry enough to kill you for it."

"That makes sense though. If we're undercover and—"

"No." The word was so harsh, it scraped against Ian's skin.

"No, what?" He was about to hear the truth, whether he wanted to or not.

"You vanished. Disappeared. Fell off the radar a year ago, days before this op started. Days after—" Her face flushed. She strode closer and braced her hands on the back of the couch. "Ian, the team has been hunting you for a year because you're suspected of selling your hacking skills on the Dark Web to the very bad guys we've been trying to take down."

FIVE

It shouldn't have been possible for him to feel any weaker. Strength ebbed so quickly it was a wonder he didn't pitch onto the floor. Instead, he sagged in the chair.

The only strength he had left seemed to be in his hands, which gripped the recliner arms so tightly that the leather wrinkled in his grasp.

"I wouldn't." He shook his head but, even though it made the world spin, his eyes never left hers. "I would never—"

"I'd like to believe you wouldn't, but…" Her voice cracked. "Not a word. Shut down all of your tech so you couldn't be tracked." She fluttered her hand between them. "Poof."

It was clear by the way she studied his reactions that Makenzie had experience with interrogation. She evaluated him, searching for the truth.

Well, *truth* was all she'd find in him. He'd never considered going to the dark side, although he'd been offered plenty of money by bad actors to do exactly what she was saying. Betraying his team and his country wasn't something he'd do.

At least, not that he could remember.

Given the way his head was swimming, he'd probably paled at her words. She'd have to believe that was real, at least. It was a symptom no one could fake.

Not only was his mind betraying him, but his body was as well.

If they had truly been partners, then she could probably read him fairly easily. How well did she know him, exactly? At the moment, it was a lot easier to focus on their history than it was to wonder if he'd become the kind of person he typically brought to justice.

"How long were we partners?" He forced his fingers to relax on the chair arms, and the tension flowed up his arms and into his body.

"Three years." No emotion, just flat facts.

Three years. No wonder she had acted so angry and wounded at the hospital. It was likely they'd trusted one another with their lives the same way he'd trusted Gage and Makenzie had trusted Audra.

It was probably why he'd instinctively known she didn't drink coffee.

They'd have developed the ability to know what one another was thinking before they said it. They'd have shared life and death together.

He couldn't remember one second of anything they'd shared.

He closed his eyes as the guilt slammed into him again. It wasn't his fault but, man, did he feel like it was. "I'm sorry."

"What for? You drugged yourself? You're lying about your memory loss?"

"Neither." Those things he was reasonably certain about. Everything else? His life rocked more off-kilter at every moment.

This woman was the twistiest thing of all.

She was a stranger to him, yet she likely knew him better than he knew himself. "So we were...close?"

"We were good at what we did."

That was an evasive answer if there ever was one. Maybe they'd been at each other's throats for three years. That was unlikely though. In a unit like theirs, incompatibility would be addressed quickly to keep the teams working efficiently in the deep investigations they did.

Had they been closer than she wanted to admit?

The thought flamed the back of his neck. Surely not. Personal relationships between partners were a huge *nope*. More than likely, she was battling grief at being so easily forgotten by someone she knew as well as she knew herself.

Slowly, he eased out of the chair and stepped around the coffee table, closing the space between them until he stood directly in front of her. He had a couple of inches of height on her. That hadn't changed, he was sure.

His gaze kept moving, searching for something in her expression. What, he had no idea. The truth, maybe?

He shouldn't stand this close, but he also couldn't back away. Despite Ian's best judgment and his training, standing close to Makenzie Fuller kick-started his emotions. They rocked his shaky balance, and he stepped back. "If we were partners for that long, then we know each other better than some married couples do. You should know I'd never do something illegal." He backed up another step and wavered. "Or did I?"

The uncertainty on her face gutted him.

"What was the evidence?" He needed proof, even if it worked against him.

"Mostly circumstantial. You disappeared. A new hacker showed up on the scene shortly after. You were in…" She balled her fists. "Look, I talked to Major Tangaro while you were with the doctor. At the very least, you're wanted for desertion. The chain of command wants to talk to you, and you're in my custody until I can close this investigation."

Exhaustion slammed him like a semi-truck. "I'm sure they have questions," he muttered and kneaded his temple, then stepped around her to the hallway. Right now, he had no answers, and he couldn't handle another dose of truth. "Is there any reason I shouldn't sleep? Anything the doctor said?"

Makenzie shook her head. "You don't have a head injury. All of this is drug induced and will hopefully wear off with some rest."

"My room is on the right?"

"Yes. And if you want to change, I…" She looked away. "I left your go bag where put it when we were planning the op."

Why would she do that? If he wouldn't need the safe house, why leave his stuff behind?

Maybe it was emotional, and he really had hurt her.

But he was too tired to think about that now. Ian walked up the hall and into the room. He shut the door and dragged a hand down his cheek, scrubbing against stubble.

Although the world was steadier, his knees still felt like rubber bands and his head still throbbed. It was like going to concerts in college and standing near the bass speakers. The thumping took over everything, even seemed to control his heartbeat.

Not that he'd cared at twenty. If he tried to headbang now at thirty-five, it would probably kill him.

He winced, then headed for the closet. If Makenzie was telling the truth and they had been partners who set up this safe house together, that go-bag would be filled with his clothes and some personal items. His backup weapon.

Not that he felt like he truly needed it. It would make him feel better to have a way to defend himself though. Everything about this night made him feel vulnerable, from waking up in a hospital bed, to the backless gown, to being shoved around in a wheelchair while Makenzie protected him.

Sure, she was capable, but so was he. He'd felt like a helpless child being pushed in his mommy's stroller.

He gripped the handle of the folding closet door and hesitated. If it was empty, then Makenzie was lying and he had even bigger problems than he'd already imagined. He didn't think she had turned on the team or on him, but he also couldn't remember what he'd had for breakfast.

Clearly, he wasn't the greatest judge.

Sliding the door open slowly, he scanned the floor.

A dark gray backpack leaned against the wall. The side pocket hung open.

That was his bag, all right. Gage had given it to him early on in his tenure on the team. Said that it was better than the army-issued ones. *More pockets. Less weight.*

The man had been obsessive about pockets.

If only Gage was here now. At least he'd have someone he could *remember* trusting.

It was clear the bag had been searched at some point, likely after he left. His backup pistol was gone as were the credentials he'd have kept inside. So the unit had searched for clues here, and then Makenzie had left his stuff? It made no sense.

Anger blazed but, just as quickly, it flamed out. The team had been following protocol. Given the circumstances and the accusations swirling around him, digging through his personal effects was wise.

That didn't make the burn any less.

It was hard to determine who was more trustworthy, Makenzie or this four-years-ago version of himself. The uncertainty shuddered anxiety through him.

He gripped the closet door and wrestled the wave of fear that threatened to drown him. He couldn't be certain of anything, not even his own identity.

Breathing in and out slowly, Ian forced the wave to ebb. He needed to find something of himself.

That started with getting out of this borrowed set of a stranger's clothes.

A quick shower and a date with a toothbrush helped, although both took longer than they should have. Changing into jeans and a dark gray long-sleeved tee helped even more. Clothes he recognized made him feel less like a lost puppy.

The cleanup also left him exhausted.

He crept around the room, touching things, investigating, trying to remember being here in the past.

The bed was made. The drawers were empty. A heavy metal baseball bat rested in the corner near the window. He hefted it, then set it back into place. Clearly, Makenzie wasn't concerned about him attacking her with that. She probably realized he was too weak to do much damage.

Wasn't she worried he'd break a window? He parted the curtain. The windows didn't open. They were single-paned glass, common on older houses like this one. A well-placed blow to the bottom corner would shatter the entire pane of glass.

His eyes traced the frame.

Yep. Breakage sensors. They'd sound the alarm fast.

Good thing he no longer felt the need to run. For now.

In his current condition, he wouldn't get very far anyway. Cupping his hands on the glass, he peered into the night. Dark shadows of the trees indicated that the land sloped upward quickly from the narrow yard.

Nope. He wasn't going anywhere.

Letting the curtains fall, he scanned the room again. Nothing sparked a memory or even a vague sense that he'd seen the place before. It bore his fingerprints though. The go bag... He'd used the same one for years. He could remember packing it before previous operations. Even down to the extra pair of thick socks tucked into an inside pocket. After basic training, he'd vowed never to suffer with wet feet again.

The small Bible in a plastic baggie in the main compartment of the backpack was his as well. Good for reading when time stretched long. Good for refreshing when the job made him weary.

He flipped through the thin pages. The underlined passages and notes were all his. He clearly remembered sitting at his kitchen table, marking verses he thought might help bolster him if he ever had to go on the run.

He needed that strength now. Flipping

to Genesis 16, he scanned the verses in Hagar's story, when she called God "him that seeth me." That was a certainty, even as everything else wavered.

Too bad there weren't verses about what to do when someone tried to kill you and made you forget a chunk of your life.

Sliding the Book into the pocket, he settled the bag on the floor by the nightstand and lay down.

When the room spun, he propped up on two pillows and tried again. His body relaxed. *Finally.*

He shut off the light and stared at the dark ceiling, willing away imagined monsters hiding in the shadows.

There were more than enough monsters in his real life.

If Makenzie was telling the truth, one of the worst might be himself.

Stepping quietly along the hardwood, Makenzie stared up the hall at Ian's closed door, gripping her backup cell. A "dumb phone," it had no GPS, no web browser, and no capabilities outside text and voice calls.

She could report in, but Major Tangaro had ordered her to limit communication until the op was over.

It wasn't over. She'd been storing intel on a secure cloud server that only she could access. All of Butler's tech—and hers—was still at the castle. She needed to retrieve it before someone else did. If she could crack that new device Storm had provided...

She'd need someone with Ian's skills for that. While he seemed to be telling the truth, she wasn't ready to trust him with a computer. He had the kind of abilities that would let him shut down the power grid. Handing him a laptop would be foolish.

Besides, she had more control now than she'd had in months. Just having her credentials again made her feel more capable. She'd tucked them in her back pocket after she dug them out of their hiding place, a security blanket of sorts.

Ian wouldn't find credentials or a weapon in his bag. Overwatch had searched it the day after he vanished. But Makenzie had asked them to leave it behind. At that moment, she couldn't bear to think he'd never come back.

But had he truly returned now?

Lord, You know if Ian's innocent and telling the truth. Could You clue me in?

She hadn't talked much to God on this op. Talking to Him highlighted the split between her real self and the role she was playing in a way that made her feel like she was two different people.

But she'd never lost sight of Him being with her.

She was especially grateful for His presence tonight. They were safe, and Ian was secured. The windows in the bedrooms were single panes of glass wired with multiple sensors. He wasn't going anywhere.

Maybe he'd rest. Sleep might help him recover his balance and possibly his memory.

Balance? It was a fair guess she might never again feel balanced herself.

Sinking to the arm of the couch, she never looked away from his door.

Ian was right. She did know him well. Maybe too well. The Ian she'd known would never do what he was suspected of.

In some strange twist, the Ian in front of her was still that Ian, at least until he recovered his memory. He was his four-years-ago self.

When he became his present-day self again, would he be the man who'd been her partner? The man she'd been falling in love with?

She shook her shoulders, throwing off the memory and the emotions. They didn't belong on this op or in this moment.

When he recovered his memory, he might be someone she didn't even recognize.

As her neck started to ache, she decided she'd been sitting too long. Rather than let her brain roam around looking for answers she'd never know for sure, she'd do better to make certain the house was secure, then try to rest.

She roamed the house, checking doors and windows and arming the security system. There was only one way into the house without busting windows. Dropping onto the couch, Makenzie laid the phone beside her and faced the door, making sure her gun was within reach.

She'd doze like she'd done on more than one stakeout while Ian kept watch. Asleep enough to rest. Awake enough to hear if anyone tried to get in.

Or out.

Closing her eyes, she leaned her head against the back of the couch. Did she believe him?

Yes.

Her head screamed that she shouldn't. If he was guilty, then he knew he was in trouble. He'd pull out all of the stops to get away again or to save his skin.

If he was innocent, why would Butler want him dead?

Was Ian helping another bad actor hack Butler's associate? Or was he working to take them down?

Alone? Vigilante style? Why? In all the years they'd worked together, in every professional and personal conversation, Ian had never brought up a need for revenge against anyone. His others-focused heart was one of the reasons she'd fallen for him. Exhaustion took the brakes off her memories.

Of the first time she'd realized he was more than a professional partner to her, when he took her hand while she was telling him about the betrayal of her soccer coaches in high school and college. Of the toll it had taken on her ability to trust. There had been a softening in his expression, a kind of awe when he'd realized she trusted him.

She'd almost kissed him that day, while they were eating lunch at a waterfront table in Savannah.

Six months later, he'd admitted that day had shifted something inside him, too. They'd finally shared that first kiss.

Then he'd walked away. He'd betrayed her, knowing it would cut her.

So while she wanted to believe him, she...

Jolting upright, Makenzie grabbed her

pistol and leaped to her feet, heart pounding. She blinked against the brightness of the table lamps and glanced at her watch.

Nearly five in the morning. How had she managed to sleep so hard?

Worse, what had jerked her into the real world?

Holding her Sig low, she strained to hear anything out of place. Her sleep-fogged brain dragged two steps behind her senses.

Silence reigned.

Holstering her pistol, she padded up the hall to listen at Ian's door. His light snore said he was still asleep, so it wasn't anything he'd done to startle her awake.

She went to the kitchen and drained the remainder of a bottle of water that still sat on the counter.

Man, her mouth was dry. She'd better not have snored. If she had and Ian heard her, she'd never catch the end—

A soft pop.

The lights blinked off.

Darkness fell, complete and heavy to her light-blinded eyes.

Pistol in hand, Makenzie faced the door and tried to slow her breathing and her thoughts. Someone had found them. They had to get out or fight.

Since the electrical panel was downstairs in the garage, she probably had thirty seconds to block the door before whoever had killed the power came blasting in.

And they probably had on night-vision goggles.

Muscle memory got her to the heavy TV stand beside the door. Bracing her back against the side, she leveraged her feet against the floor and pushed. The heavy furniture that had been placed there for just this moment shifted, slid.

The stairs to the deck creaked.

Someone was coming up. Slowly. Stealthily.

With one last shove, she blocked the door. That would stop them, but only for about thirty seconds.

Eyes adjusting enough to make out dim shapes, she jogged toward the hallway. She had to wake Ian. If it seemed they were outgunned, they would bust the bedroom window and make their way—

A loud bang tripped her footsteps.

The floor-to-ceiling windows shattered.

Glass rained on the hardwood.

Taking a knee at the end of the couch, Makenzie aimed, counting shadows on the deck.

There were at least three.

Almost silently, they all rushed in.

Makenzie fired.

SIX

Ian bolted upright in bed. Where was—

Another bang rocked through the house.
A gunshot.

What—? Who was shooting in his house?
Wait.

Safe house. Amnesia. *Makenzie.*

Someone had opened fire in the house.
He was unarmed. Makenzie was protecting him.

This time, she wasn't going to do it alone.

Three more shots in a quick grouping.

He was on his feet when the bedroom
door swung open and a shadow entered.
"It's me."

Makenzie.

Ian could feel her draw closer more than
he could see her, then her hand was on his
arm. "You're going to have to break the

window. Now. I got one of them but there's at least two more coming. We have to get out before they figure out I'm no longer laying down cover fire and—"

Shouts fired in from the living room.

"They figured it out." Ian tugged on the shoes he'd dropped by the bed and headed to the window. His head was clearer and his bones less gelatinous after his sleep, but he still wasn't 100 percent. He just hoped he had enough strength to break that window.

If not, they'd die in seconds. All their assailants had to do was spray the room with bullets and it would all be over.

"I'm covering the door." Makenzie's shadow had dropped to one knee to take aim by the dresser, shielding herself from the door's direct line of sight.

Ripping the curtains off of the wall, Ian hefted the bat and swung close to the bottom corner.

The blow rattled from his hand into the center of his back. The window cracked but didn't break.

He swung again.

The window shattered in a hail of shards.

He ran the bat along the bottom edge to get any clinging glass out of the way. No one needed to cut an artery. "Let's get out—"

The door swung open, banging against the wall. Someone rushed into the room.

Makenzie fired and a male grunted and staggered backward.

He didn't go down. The shadowy figure charged forward. From the way the guy moved, it was terrifyingly clear...

He was armored up. No amount of shooting was going to permanently stop him or his buddies either.

From her hiding place, Makenzie rocketed up and drove into the man, slamming him against the wall. His head smacked the doorframe.

Another shadow entered and jerked Makenzie backward by her shirt.

Her gun clattered to the hardwood floor. "End both of them. Now." The angry words were low, and they chilled Ian to the core. This crew had shown up to finish what

Robert Butler had started with him, and now Makenzie was on their kill list as well.

Not as long as he had breath in him.

As Ian stepped closer, Makenzie struggled with her captor. She arched her back suddenly, slamming her head into the man's face.

With a cry, he dropped her and bent double.

When the second man reached for her, Ian swung the baseball bat, connecting with a force that rattled his shoulder.

The man dropped as though his muscles had liquefied.

Ian reached down and grabbed Makenzie's arm, hauling her up. "Let's go."

Shaking her head like a dog trying to clear itself of water, she followed him to the window.

They hit the ground and ducked beneath the windowsill. Outside, the stars offered a bit more light.

Makenzie motioned to the left and headed across the narrow, moss-covered yard, plunging into the deeper darkness beyond the tree line.

Moving away from the house was the only way they were going to survive. Still holding the bat, Ian trailed behind her, ears tuned in to anything happening at the house.

Someone shouted, but he couldn't make out words over the blood rushing in his ears.

He was flagging quickly. He'd pushed too hard, but they had no choice. Sleep had given the drugs in his system some time to dissipate, but the aftereffects lingered.

He still couldn't remember what his last meal had been.

His toe caught on a tangled something as they entered the thick woods and he pitched forward, throwing out his hand and wrapping his fingers into Makenzie's shirt.

She jerked backward and stumbled into him. She made no comment but slowed the pace as they picked their way up the slope through the dark underbrush and dense trees. Makenzie seemed to be zigzagging to the left, picking their way slowly from the house and up the slope.

With every step, he tensed against imaginary bullets. This was slow going when he wanted to run.

He doubted he could.

The December air was icy. The night was eerily quiet. Their footsteps sounded like cannons in the brittle air. If their attackers stopped to listen, they'd find the trail in no time.

After a few minutes that felt like weeks, Makenzie crouched behind a fallen tree, watching the direction from which they'd come.

Ian settled beside her and leaned forward, resting his head against the damp wood, trying to regain his balance, physically and mentally.

"How are you holding up?"

"Better than I was." No way was he telling her that he was about five steps from dropping in his shoes. "What's the plan?" If she was half the agent she should be, she ought to have one forming. His head hurt too much to strategize.

"Truthfully? Winging it. I lost my gun in the fight. My cell is in the house. Right now, it's all about staying concealed and putting ground between us and them. I went left because natural inclination is to go right. Since they're down to two, they'll likely concentrate their search." She elbowed him in the side. "By the way, your swing is impressive."

"All-state baseball in high school." That much he remembered.

"I know."

It was unsettling that she knew more about him than he did about her. This movie his life had become held too many plot twists and not enough backstory. "Are you planning to trudge around in the dark forever?"

"Can't. It's after five. Sky will get lighter quickly. We're—" She leaned forward. "What are they doing?"

From the house, orange light flickered and expanded.

Fire.

Their attackers were torching any hope of escape. The car. Their gear. He glanced at her. "They're doing exactly what I'd do."

"Same." The grim line of Makenzie's mouth said she was thinking.

He just wished he knew what.

For a moment Makenzie was quiet, the growing flames reflecting in her eyes. "We need to get moving. We aren't far enough to be out of sight once the house goes up." Rising slowly, she proceeded a few steps then turned as Ian rose. The fire danced shadows across her face.

"What?" He followed her gaze, searching for trouble, but the silhouettes stuck close to the house, likely searching for signs of which direction they'd headed.

"There are only two men." Her voice was grim, then she turned and started trudging up the slope.

Ian watched her walk away, then looked toward the house. *Two men.*

They'd left their third, the one he'd batted in the head, to die in the inferno.

Just like Makenzie's former partner.

Turning away from the flames, he forced one foot in front of the other to catch up with Makenzie then fell in behind her, dodging tree limbs and feeling gingerly for roots and vines that could make his night even worse than it already was.

Makenzie's shoulders were rigid. Tension radiated off her, making his own physical burden even heavier.

It was tough not to put a hand on her shoulder and pull her to him. The drive to comfort her in the tortured memories was strong.

Maybe some latent part of his brain remembered the trust of their partnership after all?

Losing her first partner so violently had to be horrific. He couldn't imagine. "Mak, I know what you're thinking."

She stumbled and righted herself, then stepped around a protruding limb. "I'm thinking that if we follow the curve of the hill and make our way over that ridge, then head east down the other side, we'll eventually make it to the main road to Flat Rock. From there I've... I've got someone I can call. It's not ideal, but it should be safe for the moment." She picked up the pace. "That's all I'm thinking."

"Really?"

She moved forward as though she hadn't heard the question.

It had grown darker in the woods as the thick trees and undergrowth masked the flames. He couldn't see the house any longer, just a hazy glow through the trees. In the distance, sirens wailed.

"That ought to chase off our bad guys." Makenzie's pace amped up another notch, almost too fast for the conditions and the darkness. The forest was thick. They were running on dim light.

"I can't go as fast as you're charging right now." Not with his body still in recovery mode and the pain from the car accident starting to rack through him.

This was humiliating.

Makenzie slowed but didn't stop. "Sorry." She was a woman on a mission, bent on getting them to safety… Or outrunning her own emotions.

He couldn't let her do that. "You're thinking about Audra."

Makenzie stopped so fast Ian nearly ran into her. He managed not to only by grabbing a tree trunk beside him.

"Actually, I'm not." As the sirens grew louder, she turned toward him. The shifting shadows made her look menacing, but the pain in her eyes took the edge off the threat. "Then what's wrong?"

Drawing her lip between her teeth, Makenzie shook her head and looked over his shoulder, in the direction of the burning house. She opened her mouth. Closed it. Tightened her jaw. With narrowed eyes, she studied his face almost as though she could read his mind.

She was wondering whether or not she could trust him.

Finally, she sighed and her expression set into one he recognized from earlier. She was in work mode. "Butler's men found you at the hospital. No big deal. They could have followed the ambulance or deduced where you were taken. It's the nearest trauma center. But Ian?" Her expression tightened. "They were claiming to be from our unit."

The breath left his lungs in a rush, and his grip on the tree tightened. "Our top-secret unit." A unit few people even knew existed. Because they often investigated those who investigated others, their existence was on a need-to-know basis.

"The safe house is owned by an identity created within Eagle Overwatch. No one outside of the unit would know it exists."

Ian tipped his head toward the sky, but the way the limbs and stars spun, he immediately wished he hadn't.

Because that spinning swirled in with a dawning realization.

Whoever wanted him dead wasn't just someone in Robert Butler's organization.

It was someone they trusted.

Surely days had passed since she'd first spotted Ian at that wedding.

The clock said it had only been twelve hours.

Settling into the passenger seat of her father's pickup truck, Makenzie closed her eyes and tried to avoid looking out the rear window for a tail. James Fuller was perfectly capable of keeping an eye on the road behind them. A retired intel analyst with the CIA and a former SEAL, he was adept at escape and evasion.

Having her father come to their rescue was not her most stellar idea, but it was all Makenzie had. They needed a place to rest with someone watching their backs. To gear up and make a plan. While it was possible for someone to find them there, it would be difficult. Her father's address wasn't listed as her home of record, and her next-of-kin info was buried deep.

If she was right and these attacks were spurred on by someone on their team, her hiding places were limited, and she couldn't contact her team for aid. Not until she knew what was happening. With Audra's death ever fresh in her mind, she had to wonder...

Was someone in the unit playing for the wrong team? Someone who wasn't Ian? If they were, who was left that she could trust?

The biggest question that she still needed to answer... Could she trust Ian?

He rode behind her, hopefully resting from their flight into Flat Rock. She'd had to borrow a cell phone off an early morning jogger they'd met on the road and had dialed up her dad. He lived a couple of hours away, north of Asheville on a commercial Christmas tree farm and apple orchard.

"You're awfully quiet over there." Her dad's Texas drawl shone through. When he was on the job, he'd worked to mitigate the twang, but retirement had brought the real him to life, accent and all.

"Just thinking." Her father was her most trusted confidant, although her twin brother was a close second. At one time, Ian had been right in the mix with them. "I wish you had told me sooner that Zane and Noah were at the farm. I'd have reconsidered hiding out there." Her brother was home on leave with her six-year-old nephew for the holidays. Zane's wife, Chelsea, was on an unaccompanied tour in South Korea and wouldn't be joining them for Christmas. "I don't want to risk putting Noah in danger."

"He'll be fine. Between me, you, Ian, and your navy SEAL brother, he's safer than he'd be anywhere else in the world."

"Still…" It didn't sit well with her. "We'll have to move on quickly, before anyone figures out where we are."

"Take your time. Plan well." He kneaded the steering wheel with hands roughened by pine sap and hard work. "You have any idea where you're headed? When you'll stop running?"

Makenzie shook her head and shifted her eyes toward the back seat. For now, she didn't want to talk in front of Ian. Too much uncertainty kept her wary.

Her dad chuckled. "He's been racked out for the last ten miles."

Really? The leather seat creaked as Makenzie looked over her shoulder. Sure enough, Ian was close-lidded and slack-jawed. The complete relaxation in his body left no doubt his slumber was real. "Maybe this will let the last of whatever he was dosed with break down in his system."

"And restore his memory?"

"If he's actually lost it." She murmured her suspicion and turned to look out the front windshield. They'd been on the road for a while, and the highway traffic was growing sparse. They'd left Asheville behind with all of its last-minute holiday shoppers and craft fairs, winding deeper into the Blue Ridge Mountains, which were earning their name today. In the low-hanging mist and the watery sunshine, they held the blue cast that made them famous.

"For what it's worth, I believe him." Her dad glanced in the rearview then at her. "A man can fake a lot of things, but the way he looks at you now is a whole lot different than the way he used to look at—"

"You can stop, Dad. The past is dead." They weren't wandering this conversational trail today. Not when so much was in flux and she was still adjusting to his reappearance.

The Ian she'd known and cared for had walked away. The one who might have been more than a partner had abandoned and betrayed her.

There had been too much of that in her life.

She'd bitten down on her attraction to him for months after it began to grow. It was dangerous. Falling for your partner was a cliché, and it was frowned upon. It led to bad decisions in the heat of battle.

When Ian had kissed her... When they'd decided to move forward with a personal relationship while they shifted their roles on the team...

That's when she'd handed him her heart.

He'd walked away. Further proof that trusting others was a terrible choice.

Their past might be the reason that the Bad Idea Fairy seemed to have taken up residence in her head ever since she saw his face the night before. Emotions were driving her decision-making.

That had to stop.

Watching firs and pines pass, she slid her

still-cold hands beneath her thighs, letting the heated seat warm her numb fingers. "There's too many questions about why he disappeared."

"All conjecture." Her dad checked the rearview again, probably gauging whether Ian was still oblivious to the world around him. "What do you *really* think is the truth?"

She couldn't lie to her dad. Had never been able to. Even as a teenager, when her friends had frequently skipped school, she hadn't dared try. Maybe it was their close relationship in the wake of her mother's death. Maybe it was his training. Whatever it was, he could read her like an open book.

Resting her elbow on the door, Makenzie propped her head up and watched her father from the corner of her eye. "Honestly?"

"Well, I don't want you to lie."

She almost smiled. He recognized her stalling tactics. "It never made sense to me." For the first time, she voiced the truth out loud, the one that had chased her thoughts since the day Ian vanished. "Ian was that guy who… Well, you know." Ian had spent more than one vacation on the farm with her family. Having grown up in foster care, he'd never had a family to go home to, so once they became close, he'd tagged along to visit hers. Since she'd often brought Audra along as well, years before, her father had often teased her about adopting the "strays."

"Ian was honest to a fault." Her dad carefully watched the road that wound up toward the farm. "Nothing he was accused of ever set with me either."

"I worked with him every day. We spent more off hours together than most teammates do. Even before we told each other—" *Yeah, not discussing that.* She changed course. "He was my closest friend for years, and there was never anything suspicious. He never threw money around. Never took any odd phone calls. Never got super protective of his tech the way people do when they're hiding something. Nothing that would make me think he was turning."

"Until he walked away."

"Like that." Snapping her fingers, Makenzie straightened as they neared the turnoff to the farm. Slightly paranoid thanks to his past, her father had made certain there was only one way in and one way out of his property.

While part of the commercial farm was accessible to the trucks that hauled apples, pines and firs to stores across the country, dense forest and high fences surrounded the acreage nearest the house. Alarms and cameras kept watch day and night. Even if someone figured out where she'd fled, it would be nearly impossible to reach them.

"Maybe you should ask him." Her father's words bounced with a dip in the gravel road.

"I have, but apparently any memories of me have evaporated." She braced as the truck slowed and made the turn into the narrow dirt lane, then stopped to wait for the gate to slide open. "According to him, it's four years ago. Gage's his partner. I'm the new kid."

"Have you tried reaching out to Gage?

Seeing if he can talk to Ian? Maybe get to the truth?"

The truck rolled along the pine-needle-and-packed-dirt drive that wound through the forest to the main house. "You don't *find* Gage. He's off the grid. Occasionally, he reaches out, but not often. The last time he contacted any of us, he was somewhere near the Marshall Islands in the Pacific. That was months ago. When he took off in his boat, he left everything behind." Ian had grieved that cut for a long time, which made it even more painful that he'd done almost the same to her.

"Kind of like you thought about doing when Audra was murdered?"

Her father should know. She'd cried on his shoulder, unburdening herself of the sights and sounds and smells of that awful day. The ferocity of the murder and its aftermath led most to believe the attack was somehow personal.

Though no one could figure out why. The arms dealer they'd taken down had tipped her hand with Audra's death and had been put away for life, proclaiming her innocence all the way. It had seemed like overkill to murder her so viciously simply because she discovered Audra was an undercover agent.

Criminals rarely acted rationally.

Today, though, new light was beginning to dawn like the sun rising over the mountains. "Dad, what if someone really is dirty in the unit? Not just on my team in Maryland, but even higher than that? What if they were involved in Audra's death? How do I—"

"Take a deep breath." As the truck coasted to a stop near the farmhouse, her father laid a hand on her shoulder as though he could press Pause on her thoughts. A quick squeeze, then he shifted the truck into Park and killed the engine. "Right now, you need rest."

He didn't understand. She had too much to process. To plan. Rest would have to wait.

"When you were a kid..." His chuckle was deep. "You'd get tired, and do what your mother called *spiraling*. Remember that?"

Makenzie dug her teeth into her lower lip. Yeah. She remembered.

But she wasn't a kid anymore.

"That doesn't stop just because you grow up. All of us can get trapped in our wild thoughts or start thinking with our emotions. You've been trained to rest, then plan. Use your training." All amusement faded, and his eyes grew dark. "In a job like yours, you sleep when you can, because you never know when the next respite will come."

Nodding slowly, Makenzie reached for the door handle.

Her father's hand on her back stopped her. "Mak, listen." His voice dropped too low for Ian to hear if he happened to wake up. "You've been undercover for a year. It takes a toll. Let yourself process. Rest and find yourself again. You're safe here."

With those words, she was fifteen years old, angry at her mother for dying of cancer and longing for security in a world gone mad.

Her father was right. She needed to take the quiet while she could get it. Danger was sure to make another charge.

SEVEN

He'd been here before.

Leaning against the side of the truck, Ian studied the three-story house from lawn to weathervane. He sorted through memories like flipping through a deck of cards, but none matched the stone first floor or the cedar logs that made up the second and third levels. The huge wraparound decks and the windows set high in the peak of the roof didn't pair with any specific memory.

The house simply generated a feeling in his stomach. One that was warm and electric. A shot of adrenaline that wasn't about fleeing for his life but about expectation.

He gritted his teeth in frustration.

The harder he tried to pin the feeling to a concrete thought, the more his body tensed and the more his brain fogged. How did four years simply not exist?

If he hadn't been in an actual hospital and heard the diagnosis from a real doctor, he'd think this was all some wild setup. That Makenzie Fuller was lying.

Maybe she was. This could all be an elaborate scheme to get him to...

To what end? He couldn't come up with a motive to such a scheme.

Those men at the hospital and at the safe house had been very real and had pulled no punches with Makenzie. While she could be a bad actor, the evidence wasn't there.

Either he believed her or he didn't.

Seeing as how she'd placed herself literally in the line of fire for him more than once, he was compelled to think she was telling the truth.

He was also compelled to trust his gut. The deepest parts of himself wouldn't steer him wrong and, while he felt no specific recognition, he had definitely been here before. If only he knew how he knew that.

"You okay?" Makenzie appeared and

leaned against the truck a few feet away from him. She held a picture frame, which she turned over and over in her hands.

He wasn't sure where she'd come from, but she definitely shouldn't have been able to sneak up on him. If he was going to get out of this alive, he needed to put his head on straight.

Wait. *Head on straight...*

He tilted his head from one side to the other again, then smiled. It was the first real joy he'd felt since opening his eyes in the hospital. He wanted to swim in it.

She eyed him warily. "What?"

His grin widened, even though it felt like a stupidly small thing to be happy about. "I did this..." He repeated the move, tipping his head. "And this." A tip to the other side. "And the world didn't flop around like a fish on a hook."

Makenzie's eyebrows rose in approval. "That's awesome. Any memories come along with that trick?"

"No, but I've been here before, haven't I?"

With a sniff, Makenzie turned and stared

up at the house, which sat on a low rise in a clearing surrounded by tall trees.

It was a perfect defensive position. Nobody would be able to make their way out of the tree line without being seen. The high windows let light in without allowing a line of sight from the outside.

Smart.

When Makenzie finally answered, she directed the words toward the house. "You have. Many times." She held out the picture frame. "I thought you might like some proof about…about us."

He took the frame, but he kept his eyes on hers. She still looked sad. It made him want to apologize, but he didn't know what for.

Instead, he turned the frame over. In the photo, he stood on the deck above them, his arm draped casually around Makenzie's shoulders. She was laughing as she looked at the camera, her joy contagious enough to draw a smile.

The Ian in the photo was looking at her.

Part of his career involved reading people, and if he had been looking at this photo from the outside, he'd think that man cared about that woman.

Enough to look at her like his world centered around her.

He'd never look at his partner that way.

Maybe it was a trick of the light. An odd expression of humor.

Regardless, here was proof that she was being truthful, at least about some things. He returned the photo. "Did I visit a lot?" Gage had been a good friend as well as a teammate. While he'd often hung out at Gage's apartment, he'd never traveled to Indiana to meet the man's family.

Then again, he'd never looked at Gage the way he was looking at Makenzie in that photo, either.

She held the picture to her chest. "You liked my family. They liked you. You spent as much time here as I did. You went fly fishing with my dad once when I couldn't get away." Without looking at him, she shoved away from the truck and headed toward the house, stopping a few feet away. "We should rest. If that nap you took in the truck helped, maybe deeper sleep will help more."

It wasn't even midmorning, but she might be right. He'd slept fitfully at the safe house. Maybe here he could find healing. More healing might bring—

What did she just say? He closed the gap between them and grabbed her elbow before he considered the action. Turning her gently, he dipped his head and forced her to look him in the eye. "You said I might regain more memories. So you believe I don't remember?" Earlier she'd been certain that he was lying. If she was truly hearing him now, maybe she'd eventually trust him.

Unless he really had become a man unworthy of that trust.

Her eyes scanned his, deep and serious and wounded. Something he'd done in the past had hurt her. If only he knew what.

Or maybe he'd rather keep forgetting.

Gently, she extracted her elbow from his grasp. "I'm choosing to believe you. Don't make me regret it."

His hand drifted toward her again, but

when she took another step away, he dropped it. "I really am sorry that I don't remember. Gage and I are... Were? We were tight. Friends as well as partners. If he suddenly forgot me?" That kind of grief defied words. "It would hurt."

Pain flashed on her face. She nodded and turned toward the house. "I'm starving and Dad's making bacon and eggs. We're safe here. The security measures are top-notch."

"After that?"

"I don't know. I'm going to rest, then there's some evidence I need to retrieve."

"Where?" If she was walking into danger, he was going with her. He'd not let her fight his battles.

She held up a hand to block his questions. "Look, if I'm right, then I can't take you to Maryland or reach out to our team. Not yet. Someone wants you dead. If it's someone in Overwatch?" Biting her lip, she shook her head. "I won't be responsible for that."

She did that a lot, worried her lip with her teeth. Seemed to be a nervous habit, one he probably ought to remember.

One that shouldn't give him the sudden, unbidden urge to press his lips against hers.

The image of himself doing just that jolted him. It was a quick burst of memory. Her in his arms. The flash of a kiss that brought a quick hit of adrenaline-fueled emotion.

It was gone as quickly as it had slammed into him.

Makenzie was at his side before he could clear his head. "What did you see?"

Instinctively, he stepped back. Was he a victim of an overactive imagination? Or at some point in time had he truly kissed his partner?

He opened his mouth, stuttered something unintelligible, then turned away before the image could reappear. Kissing her would have been the height of unprofessionalism.

If the look on his face in that photo was real…

"Ian?"

No way could he tell her what he'd seen. "Nothing. It was nothing. You're right. I need to rest. Get my head on straight. Remember who I am."

And who exactly Makenzie Fuller was to him.

Her body rebelled against sleeping while the sun was in the sky.

And while she had more questions than answers about everything in her life.

Carrying her third cup of tea, Makenzie gripped a legal pad and stepped onto the upstairs deck. The house had been built like a vacation home, living area upstairs and bedrooms on the floor below, so that maximum views could be shared by all.

It was colder on the deck, away from the oversize fireplace and the overdone Christmas tree draped in lights, but she needed space more than warmth. Thick wool socks and a sweater from the closet in her old room helped ward off the chill…a little.

Settling into an Adirondack chair, she dropped the legal pad into her lap and cradled the thick ceramic mug in her palms.

She squinted against the noon sun. On the hilltop, no shade blocked the glare.

With a full stomach and enough caffeine in her system to power a city block, she finally felt capable of puzzling out what came next.

Picking up the pen, she set her tea on the chair's wide arm and drew her feet beneath her. As she doodled snowmen in the top margin, she let her mind wander over the past eighteen hours then drift through the past twelve months. Free thinking usually dropped puzzle pieces into place.

All it did today was scatter the pieces across the table. They simply didn't connect in a way that made sense. The picture pointed to Ian angering Robert Butler.

Because of Storm?

Butler had been a powerful arms dealer, but he hadn't gone international, although it was in his plans. Storm would help him do that.

She'd learned a lot about Butler in a year. His transactions were in cryptocurrency, which was notoriously difficult to track.

If someone wanted weapons, a network of in-person sources bounced the message up the chain until it reached him. The lines of communication were tough to trace.

Even as his personal bodyguard, Makenzie hadn't cracked access to the entire system. She'd been close though.

Now Butler was dead. A year of undercover work was slipping away, and she needed to get to the castle to retrieve what she could. She'd called as her undercover persona and requested Butler's room and hers be left untouched until she could get there. All she needed to do now was wait for the rest of the guests to clear out.

"You're doodling. That means something big is brewing." The deep voice behind her didn't surprise her. Her twin brother had always known when she was spun up and needed a sounding board.

Where she was a free-form thinker, Zane was a lists and charts guy. Where she was the dark brunette image of her father's mountain heritage, Zane was the blond representation of their mother's Eastern European ancestors. They couldn't look or think more differently if they were strangers. That they were twins shocked everyone.

Dragging an Adirondack chair closer, Zane sat and turned his face toward the sun. "How are you handling all of this?"

"I'm fine." She looked over her shoulder. Where his dad was, Noah was usually close behind. "Where's my nephew?"

"Riding the four-wheeler with Dad. We figured you'd have a better chance of getting sleep if he wasn't banging on your door."

It felt good to smile. Noah's greeting when she'd walked into the house had been exuberant. She hadn't seen him since she last visited them in Norfolk just before she went undercover.

He'd greeted Ian with the same excitement. Thankfully, Ian had played along, but his confused expression made it clear he had no memory of the boy.

Zane shifted in the chair. Nobody ever believed he was a SEAL. He didn't fit the broad-shouldered, square-jawed movie version. Tall and slim, Zane looked like the word nerd that Makenzie could be. That probably worked to his advantage more often than he'd ever tell. "Christmas is in five days."

"I know." Nobody could fault her for not being in the spirit. Not with all that was happening around her.

"So are you staying?" Without lifting his head, he turned his face toward her.

Between deployments and ops, it had been years since the family had been together for Christmas. Noah had probably been two the last time. With Zane serving as a radio operator with the SEALs and his wife also active duty in the navy, coordinating leave wasn't easy.

Well, she couldn't promise him this year either. "Dad hasn't told you?"

"Just that Ian has no memory of the past four years because someone tried to kill him."

"Yeah, well, it's bigger than that." She sketched out as much as she could without violating the secrecy of her blown mission. "I don't know what to do next."

"Who do you suspect?" He reached for her notepad and she passed it over, although it contained nothing but her doodles and a handful of names.

His head snapped up. "You have your commander on this list."

Yeah. That one had gutted her, too. "She's the only one I talked to when we were at the hospital. Unless someone was tracking my phone—"

"Or planted a tracker on Ian."

"Everything he had on him when I found him was left behind at the hospital. He wasn't what led them to the safe house."

Zane flipped to the second page, which was blank, then let it fall. "You don't have your phone on you, do you?"

"I'm not stupid." Sometimes the old sibling rivalry flared up. "No phone. No weapon. No go bag. We left everything behind."

"At least you have some clothes here." Zane scratched his cheek. "Dad's already handed Ian a stack of shirts." He grinned. "All flannel."

"Of course." Their father had taken to what they called his "farmer flannel" when he bought the land six years earlier. If he had one plaid flannel shirt, he had fifty.

Ian would look good in a blue fl—

No. Some dreams weren't hers to dream anymore.

"So about Ian…"

"Don't." Zane did not need to do that twin thing and start reading her mind. Not right now when her head was spinning so fast she almost wondered if she'd been drugged as well.

"So he doesn't remember that the two of you finally admitted how you felt about each other the last time you were here?"

There it was. Out loud. "A lot has happened since then." He'd disappeared less than a week later. Despite their promises and plans.

If any of it had been real for him.

He'd tagged along with her to the farm to visit her family before their undercover mission in the Butler organization dropped them off the radar. She was to go in as boots on the ground. He'd be intel and help on the outside.

They'd tap-danced around their feelings for a while. Had been wildly reasonable about it all.

Until that moment down by the pond.

That kiss her brother had interrupted by the pond? It had finally sealed a promise.

"We said a lot that day." Makenzie swallowed. "Yes, we kissed. Maybe it was Christmas spirit out of hand." It had been so much more than that.

"Uh-huh."

Oh, how she hated that knowing, big-brother look. "Ian left me and the job. He's accused of being a criminal selling his services to the highest bidder."

She'd never truly believed it. The Ian she'd known would never.

Emma Butler would never have believed her uncle paid for her lavish wedding with ill-gotten funds either. "I rescued him from Robert Butler who called him a traitor to one of his associates. That sounds like he was working for someone." Facts ought to keep her from falling again.

"Suspicion doesn't make a man guilty." Another low voice came from behind.

This time, it wasn't someone in her family.

Makenzie gripped the arms of the chair, digging a splinter into her palm.

How much had Ian heard? *Please, God, not the kiss part.*

Ian walked around to stand in front of her and Zane, who maintained his seat. The look in her brother's eye said he was more amused about what Ian might have heard than concerned about his legal status.

Boys.

Leaning against the porch rail, Ian braced his hands behind him. "So you believe I don't remember anything, but you still think I'd sell out my country? My team?" He dipped his head. "My partner?"

"What would you think?" She stood but kept her distance. "If I vanished one day, nearly scrapped an op that was months in the planning and left you to go it alone, what would you assume? Especially when rumors—"

"Well my first assumption wouldn't be that you were a turncoat. My first assumption would be something bad happened." Shoving off of the rail, he stepped closer until he was less than an arm's length away. "Did you search for me? Wonder if I was hurt? Dead?"

She jerked her head to the side, staring at the trees that swayed gently in the December breeze as the pain of those first hours resurfaced.

Behind her, the screen door slid open, then shut.

Zane was probably wise to flee the scene.

She wished he'd stayed and played referee though. His presence might have kept her storm-tossed emotions at bay.

"Did you?" Ian leaned closer, but it wasn't a threat.

It was a plea.

When she faced him, she knew the look in his blue eyes would haunt her forever.

She could lie and pretend professional-
ism had ruled that day when, in reality,
she'd been a frantic mess, certain he was
dead. That when they entered his apartment, there would be blood.

While lying would save face for her, it
would only bring Ian more pain.

She couldn't do that. At one time, she'd
cared too much about him. Before he'd
evaporated into vapor.

Truth. Both of them needed it.

She held his gaze. "I was terrified." Her
voice was barely a whisper. The fear of that
day rested too close to the surface.

Ian's head jerked as though she'd shouted.

Now that she'd spoken, the story she'd
never told anyone refused to remain locked
away.

Tears pushed against the backs of her
eyes and residual fear clogged her throat,
holding her voice to a harsh whisper. "I
was at your apartment while they looked
for evidence of blood spatter. At your car
while cadaver dogs searched. I had three
days before I had to become someone else,

to make my way into Robert Butler's good graces. I didn't sleep for any of them." Impossibly, her words shredded even more. "I was trying to find you."

Because when he'd disappeared, her heart had stopped beating. If he'd been dead…

Part of her would have died with him. That kiss had told her something she'd never realized.

That although she'd been developing feelings for her partner, those feelings had grown far beyond what she'd imagined.

Those feelings had ebbed when the evidence that he was alive and on the run came out, but banked embers of hope still glowed in her heart.

Hope that believed he couldn't have turned on her or on his team.

Hope that flamed higher as he closed the gap between them, his expression guarded as he searched her face.

Her heart almost cracked her rib cage. She shouldn't let him do this.

She couldn't stop him either. Her hand lifted on its own accord and rested on his chest, where his heart pounded against her palm, as wild and unleashed as her own.

As suddenly as he'd moved closer, he tore his gaze from hers, staring over her shoulder.

With a deep breath, he closed his eyes, then stepped around her and walked away.

EIGHT

The sound of an ax thudding against dead wood rang through the trees. The impact rattled Ian's hands and raced up his arms into his shoulders, a burning ache that quaked all the way into his brain.

Maybe it would rattle something loose.

Twisting the ax head, he pulled it free from the dead apple tree and swung again.

This would be easier with the chain saw Zane had offered, but he needed physical labor to remind him he wasn't weak. He wasn't who Makenzie believed he was.

Okay, to be honest, he needed to rattle the fact he'd once kissed her right out of his skull. Hearing her talking to Zane had nearly driven him backward with the shock.

He'd nearly kissed her again today. Right

on the deck of her father's house in front of God and everybody.

Jerking the ax free, he struck the tree again.

At some point after his memories slammed into a brick wall, they'd shared something bigger.

If she was his partner, what had happened? That wasn't how it worked. In fact, a romance with the person you had to rely on to make hard decisions when the bullets started flying was the worst thing an investigator could do.

It might explain some of the odd feelings she brought up. Feelings that even the holes in his Swiss-cheesed memory couldn't filter out.

He swung again, the ring of the ax and the strike of the blow working to shake the tension from his nerves.

"You know, I own about six chain saws. I'd be happy to run to the barn and bring one down to you."

Leaving the ax in the tree stump, Ian turned to find Makenzie's father watching from a few feet away. James Fuller leaned against the fence that ran along the edge of the row, his hands shoved in his pockets. Even though he was dressed in an orange flannel shirt, jeans and a heavy work jacket, he still carried himself with the air of federal agent.

And this one was sizing up a suspect.

How long had he been standing there? Ian freed the ax from the tree and tried to look, well, *normal*. Whatever that was. "I thought you were riding the four-wheeler with your grandson."

"Noah?" James narrowed his eyes, but it was more question than suspicion.

Noah. "I should know him, shouldn't I?"

"You two were the best of friends the first time he met you, so I'd be careful about letting him know you don't remember him. Grown-ups are struggling with this. A six-year-old definitely would."

Grown-ups were struggling. That meant he had been close to others in Makenzie's family who were also feeling the sting of being forgotten.

Would he ever shake this overwhelming need to apologize for something he couldn't control?

"Noah and I were out and about, but he can only handle the cold so long. I dropped him off at the barn, and Zane let me know you were down here doing his chores." Makenzie's father chuckled. "So about that chain saw?"

"No, thanks. It feels good to move. I'm just glad you had trees that needed to be taken down."

"I can imagine, given what you've been through." The older man's deep voice carried over the distance between them. "Hospital gowns and wheelchairs make a man need to prove he's still got strength in him."

Ian arched an eyebrow. "You heard about that?"

"Makenzie loves a good story."

"I wish I could remember that about her."

"You will. Eventually. There aren't that many drugs that can permanently wipe your mind. From what Makenzie tells me, while Robert Butler liked to blend his own concoctions, none of the biggies were in his arsenal."

"That's good, but I wish…" Ian leaned the ax against the tree. He wished he didn't have gaps at all. It was frustrating. A constant nagging, like trying to remember a word that was on the tip of his tongue.

Only it was his life that refused to come to him. The fight to remember was more exhausting than anything he'd ever endured. The incompleteness left him feeling tense and anxious.

"It'll come." Stepping closer, Makenzie's father stopped to inspect the low-hanging branches of the tree next to the one Ian had been taking down. "I have a feeling you've remembered a handful of things already."

Just that flash of a kiss.

No way was he confessing that to her father. Not with an ax in reach. "I've had vague feelings. Impressions. Especially since we got here."

"Well, you spent a lot of time here. After Audra died and Gage took off, you and Makenzie were both pretty wounded. The two of you took to each other in your grief. Y'all were good friends as well as partners. Given that your family is gone, you started spending holidays and downtime here. Stands to reason the farm would connect some dots." His gaze shifted, pinning Ian's as though he expected the words to bring a lightning bolt of memory.

Too bad it didn't work that way. "What are you fishing for, Mr. Fuller?" Because the man had definitely thrown a line into the water, one with a fully baited hook. "Is it about me possibly turning to the dark side?" He braced his hands on his hips. "I might not have my memory, but I know myself. That doesn't sound like me."

"I don't think it sounds like you either. And call me James, same as always."

That seemed overly familiar, but apparently he'd once known these strangers well. "How close was I to all of you?"

Tilting his head to the side, James walked closer to stand directly in front of Ian. The lines around his eyes deepened. "You were practically another son."

The words were too nonchalant. Likely, he was feeling the same kind of pain Makenzie was because of Ian's memory gaps. Caring about someone who'd forgotten you had to hurt. "I'm sorry, sir. I wish I remembered." This time, the apology wouldn't be stopped.

"Well, when you do, I'm available to talk. Until then?" James hefted the ax and held it out to Ian, handle first. "You can keep destroying your arms and shoulders with this or I can bring you a chain saw."

"This is therapeutic." Ian stared at James's face, searching for something familiar, but it simply wasn't there.

It was possible his past and these people were lost forever.

She could not get warm.

Makenzie stepped as close to the massive stone fireplace as the raised hearth would allow and shivered. She probably shouldn't have stayed on the deck so long after Ian walked away, but she'd been frozen into place by what had almost happened.

Holding her arms out, she spread her fingers and held her hands below the Christmas stockings hung on the mantel, seeking the rising heat of the wood-fueled flames. The warmth thawed her fingers, but it didn't seep into her chest.

Nope, her heart was still cold. Still tied to memories she couldn't outrun. The past had lodged in her head, swaying to the beat of "Please Come Home for Christmas" drifting in from the kitchen radio along with the spicy scent of her dad's simmering chili.

She *was* home. With Ian. On a Christmas that would have looked very different if a thousand detours hadn't derailed their *what might have been*.

The *what might have been* that had blended with the *right now* on the deck earlier.

That moment had been enough to kickstart her dormant emotions. They wouldn't be wrestled into place now.

Ian had nearly kissed her, no doubt. He'd worn that same look over a year ago. The same glint in his eye. The same parting of his lips. The same quick glance at her mouth, a silent request for permission.

Except this time, he didn't know her.

And she had no idea who was inside his wounded mind.

Eventually, Makenzie had made it to the couch in the living room before her knees gave way. She'd spent too long staring at the lights on the massive floor-to-ceiling Christmas tree, focusing until her eyes blurred the image into a giant kaleidoscope.

The past had roared. She'd replayed every conversation about walking away from their jobs in the field, him to a white-hat hacker position on the team, and her to intelligence analysis. The change would allow them to explore the thing that had been building between them almost from the moment they'd started to work together.

Something they hadn't fully acknowledged to one another until that day he'd kissed her at the pond that divided the orchard from the tree farm.

They'd agreed to press Pause. They had the Butler op in front of them, ready to roll.

Then he'd disappeared.

Both were issues now. He had no recollection of where he'd been, and she needed to get to the castle to retrieve that laptop. Her undercover persona had control of those rooms for one more day and she could get in, even if she didn't have a warrant.

That ran out tomorrow.

Or sooner if someone in the organization had wits enough to cancel their reservations when Butler died. That was doubtful, but the longer she waited, the more complicated things became.

"Aunt Mak!" Feet pounded up the stairs, chasing the shout from the lower floor where the bedrooms were.

She grinned as she turned away from the fireplace. It was like Noah knew she could use a dose of joy.

A miniature missile rocketed across the room from the stairwell, aimed straight for her. Noah wrapped his arms around her hips and looked up at her with green eyes that mirrored both hers and her brother's.

The kid was totally Zane's mini-me.

Pulling Noah's arms from around her, Makenzie dropped to her knees and let the kindergartner hug her neck to his heart's content. His puffy jacket was still cold from the outdoors.

His chilly cheek against hers warmed her heart. For the moment, she was simply *Aunt Mak*.

She backed away and eyed her nephew with an exaggerated eyebrow raise. "Why are you still wearing your coat?"

"I wanted to see if you were awake."

"Well, I'm glad you did. Here..." She pulled him away from the fireplace he'd been taught to keep a safe distance from, then helped him tug off his gloves and coat. Pulling the knitted hat straight up off of his head produced a halo of staticky hair.

Noah giggled and tried to smooth it down. "Can we have hot chocolate?"

"Sure." Standing, Makenzie handed him his outdoor gear and headed for the kitchen. "Did you have fun with Grandpa?"

"Yep. Then Dad and I went to the barn to pick out apples so Grandpa can make apple pie."

Figured. Her dad cooked when he was

working a problem. He'd taken on hers if he was making a big pot of chili and home-made apple pie.

"Where's Ian?" Noah scrambled onto a stool at the bar and thumped his palms against the marble countertop.

"He's around." If only she knew where. She grabbed two mugs and the tin of hot chocolate mix that had come from one of the local farmer's markets. Technically Ian was in her custody and she should know at all times, but on this property, he wasn't going anywhere without being spotted by cameras or motion sensors. Everything was alarmed. "I'm sure he'll be back in time for Grandpa's chili dinner. It's his favorite."

Makenzie stopped in midturn, gripping the mugs.

His favorite. So was apple pie.

She rolled her eyes. Her father couldn't help loving Ian like a son. This had to be hard on him, not existing in Ian's mind. Maybe he was hoping food would rock a memory loose.

Noah squirmed. "Ian likes apple pie?"

"I do." Ian followed his cold-roughened voice around the corner, stopping in the wide doorway from the living room. He stared at Makenzie with no expression until Noah plowed into his knees.

Ian doubled over with an exaggerated *oomph* then tickled Noah in the ribs, sending the boy into a gale of giggles.

Either Ian had recovered his memory or he was acting the part well.

When he looked at her over Noah's head, his grim expression made it clear the act was for her nephew's sake.

After a rousing tickle fight left Noah lying on the floor weak with laughter, Ian straightened and laid the side of his foot against Noah's hip, pushing him gently across the floor. "Is that your soccer ball in the yard, sir?"

Noah popped to his feet in a way Makenzie's aching body envied. "Want to play? There's a goal behind the barn."

"Maybe after lunch. Right now, your dad's looking for you downstairs. Wants you to bring your jacket down and hang it up."

Noah made an *uh-oh* face and snatched his jacket from the back of the chair, running from the room.

Makenzie shook her head as he ran out the door, the Christmas cards taped around the doorframe flapping as he passed.

His departure took the light from the room and left behind the memory of why she was here and what she had to do.

"Can I ask you a question?" Ian walked toward the bar that separated the kitchen from the breakfast nook, but he stopped halfway.

"Depends on the question."

"It's about what you said earlier."

No, he could not. If he didn't remember kissing her and making plans to explore a relationship, then... No. She wasn't going to be the one to fill him in.

"That stuff you said to your brother about me being a traitor."

She really didn't want to talk about that either, but he deserved answers. Holding up her index finger, she walked past him to the door and peeked into the den to make sure Noah had truly gone downstairs.

Only the Christmas tree showed any signs of life, its lights twinkling in the glow of the fire.

That cozy image was nothing at all like she felt on the inside, for sure.

When she turned, Ian was standing where she'd left him. Leaning against the doorframe, she crossed her arms and waited. He could drive the conversation. She didn't need to volunteer any more than necessary.

"Do you really believe I'd turn on my team and country to sell my skills to the highest bidder?" The way he asked the question said this was about more than what she believed.

Maybe he was wondering if he could trust himself.

He needed her honesty. "I don't want to believe it. For you to go turncoat would have been completely out of character." She dug her fingers into her biceps. The truth cut her as much as it would likely cut him. "We saw surveillance footage from a gas station in Des Moines, shortly before a data breach hit the Iowa payroll system. You were there."

It was as though he stopped breathing, then he shook his head. "I wouldn't have to be in town to hack a computer system."

True. Give him a two-hundred-dollar laptop and he could have the Pentagon itself on tap within minutes.

"The point is you were alive and acting on your own without reaching out to the team or to me." That had been the worst part. How could he abandon her so completely?

She reached over to the radio mounted under the cabinet and turned down "All I Want for Christmas Is You." She'd never been a fan of that song, and she certainly didn't want to think about the implications of it now. At the moment, she needed to return her focus to what she could salvage of the mission. "Look, this isn't the time to talk about it. Not with Noah in the house."

He nodded grimly.

"Anyway, I'm leaving for a few hours. You'll be safe here, and you'll also be watched closely."

He faced her head-on. Suspicion clouded his expression. "Where are you going?"

"To the castle. Butler's electronics and mine are hidden in my room there."

"Why didn't you say something sooner? Those might have everything you need to lock up your investigation. There might be something that explains why I was there."

Makenzie bit her tongue. She hadn't told him sooner because she wasn't sure she could trust him.

He stepped closer, his eyes taking on a light she recognized from past investigations. "You don't think anyone has gotten to them?"

"Doubtful. I put in a call to the manager as my undercover persona and had them secure the rooms until my return. Even if someone managed to get in, they were well hidden." How much should she tell him?

She might not know who he was the day he walked away, but she knew who he was four years ago. Upstanding. Honest. If she truly believed he'd lost his memory, then four-years-ago Ian stood before her now. She could read him in on a few details. "Butler had a second laptop he'd just started carrying. He handed it to me right before the wedding. I'd planned to dig through it after he'd done his typical party-and-pass-out routine, but other things got in the way."

"Other things like me." His eyes narrowed. "Hang on. *You* were going to hack into it?"

"That would have been your job on this op if—" She waved her hand as though he'd puffed away in a wisp of smoke.

"There's no other tech specialist who could work with you?"

"It was too late to read anyone else in and, frankly, there's never been another you." Makenzie clamped her mouth shut. That had sounded oddly romantic.

Shaking his head, Ian stalked closer, stopping just short of touching her.

His nearness drew her heart back to two hours before. To one year before.

But he didn't seem inclined to kiss her. "You're not going alone. Someone needs to watch your back." He held up his hand to stop any argument. "I'm going. I won't let you die because of me."

NINE

"Are you telling me I was almost murdered at an actual castle?" Ian leaned closer to the windshield and inspected Hopeshire Castle as Makenzie shifted the rented sedan into Park. "This is like a medieval revenge movie."

She rolled her eyes skyward. The longer they traveled in the car Zane had rented with his credit card, the more Ian had started acting like the version of himself she remembered. Likely having some semblance of control over the situation had made him more comfortable, allowing his character to make its way past the blockages in his brain.

Now at the end of their three-hour drive, his full sense of humor was in play.

Pressing the ignition, she had to wonder if bringing him was a good idea.

It probably wasn't, but it was too late to turn back now.

As she stepped out of the car, Makenzie made certain her credentials were handy. While her undercover persona could get her some level of entry into the castle's guest rooms, her badge brought more clout. Hopefully, it would buy her a look at the security footage from the wedding reception and an idea of what had precipitated Butler's attempt on Ian's life.

Of course, now she had to deal with Ian somehow believing that castle killers were oddly cooler than regular killers.

"Murdered is murdered, no matter the venue." Shutting the car door, she scanned the stone building that loomed above them. It looked as though it belonged in the European countryside instead of the Blue Ridge Mountains. The architects and builders had paid particular attention to detail, creating a modern-day fairy tale.

At least for some. All she could see was a nightmare. There were too many places to hide. Even a parapet to be shoved from.

She felt exposed and vulnerable.

The sooner they returned to the relative safety of the farm, the better.

Ian met her at the front of the vehicle. "Tell me I had a sword, even if it isn't true."

No way was she responding. Instead, Makenzie ran her hand down the dress shirt she'd dug out of the closet and hoped she looked somewhat professional. She didn't need Security calling the government for verification of her identity.

She followed the path to the office with Ian trailing her.

What if he wasn't the target? Maybe it was her. What if the murder plot had been a way for Butler to draw her out? What if Butler had been the victim of his own paranoia?

She ground her teeth together. *Her* paranoia was setting in. None of that would explain Ian's presence at the reception or who he was working for.

She shouldn't trust him, yet she did. Professionally. To a point.

As she reached for the door, he leaned

forward to whisper in her ear. "You know Inigo Montoya and the Dread Pirate Roberts had an epic sword fight in that movie—" He grunted as she elbowed his ribs.

"Are you done?" Not only did she need him to be serious, but she needed him not to stand so close that she could feel his warm breath against her skin.

She also didn't need the reminder of what "fun Ian" was like. That was the Ian she'd come dangerously close to falling in love with. The one she'd been willing to alter her career for.

"I'm done." He backed away. In the glass door, she watched him rub his side where her elbow had connected. "You're right." He straightened his shoulders and slipped into professional mode so fast Makenzie almost got whiplash. "This is serious."

Oh, how she wished it wasn't. Because if things had been different, they might have been scouting their own wedding venues. The timing would have been—

Nope. She wasn't going down that road.

Makenzie pulled the door open with force and stepped into the warm office.

Even the administrative area gave off medieval vibes, with stone walls and a massive fireplace. Elaborate woven rugs muffled their footsteps on the stone floors. Gas-lit candles fluttered in wall sconces.

The only nod to modern-day was a laptop that rested on the massive carved wooden receptionist's desk.

A middle-aged woman with long dark hair in a sleek ponytail rose from her seat behind the desk with a practiced smile. She'd helped with the planning of Emma's wedding.

Rounding the heavy wooden furniture, she held her hand out to Makenzie, who was a step ahead of Ian. "Ms. Fullerton." The undercover name almost made Makenzie wince. "We were so sorry to hear of Mr. Butler's accident on what should have been a happy occasion. How can I help you?"

Nylah Harris was as smooth and polished as she had been the day she'd led them on a tour of the property, selling the Butlers on a top-tier wedding package.

Or course she was. The full-blown event that Robert Butler had thrown for his niece had cost more than Makenzie made in a year.

Was that only the night before? It felt like years had passed.

Where were Emma and her new husband now? Or the rest of the Butler family? How had the guests reacted to Robert Butler's death?

For a moment, her heart squeezed for a young woman who had no idea that her beloved uncle had been a criminal.

Makenzie shook off the thought as quickly as she dropped Nylah Harris's hand. Emotion didn't belong here.

"Actually, my real name is Special Agent Makenzie Fuller." Reaching into her pocket, she held up her credentials for Ms. Harris to view. "This is Ian Andrews. We're here about some of the events leading up to Mr. Butler's death. I'd like to view security camera footage and regain access to the rooms I called and asked you to secure."

To Nylah Harris's credit, only a quick series of blinks indicated her surprise at Makenzie's true identity and her forthright demands. "Technically you still have access to the rooms because of the rental agreement, although the family left this morning upon learning the tragic news of Mr. Butler's death. As you requested over the phone, I made sure no one entered your room or Mr. Butler's. That falls under your contract." Her conciliatory expression shifted, hardening slightly. "But to show you security footage, I'd need a warrant."

"Actually, you don't." Makenzie slid her credentials into her pocket. "When we signed the rental agreement, we negotiated a clause that allowed us to view security footage." She'd convinced Butler it was a way she could keep an eye on guests. She'd planned to return to see if anyone had met with Butler on the side, using the wedding as a cover.

Ms. Harris started to protest, but Makenzie held up her hand. "I signed my legal name to that agreement when I was acting as Mr. Butler's representative. Since the contract is technically through Monday, I still have access. You can pull the file and discuss it with your manager. Call your legal advisor if necessary. We'll wait here."

Resetting her pleasant expression, Nylah Harris nodded and disappeared up the short hallway.

Ian appeared at Makenzie's elbow. "Smooth."

"This is not my first investigation."

"It's the first one I'm witnessing." He clicked his tongue against his teeth. "At least, it's the first one I remember. You're good."

He was standing too close again. The admiration in his voice was warming her stomach.

Or maybe she'd shoved chili in her mouth too fast as they were leaving her dad's farm.

She put distance between them before she faced him. "You lay low and don't do anything that would make them ask to see your creds." Since he was under suspicion, she'd left his identification at the farm. She'd purposely not referred to him as an agent. Hopefully, no one would notice.

Nylah reappeared, her expression a bit more gracious. "Special Agent Fuller, we can give you access to our camera footage. Would you like me to escort you to our security office?"

"No. I was there before. I'll need keys to our block of rooms though." After she'd secured the laptops, she wanted to check all of them. Hopefully Cale and the others hadn't cleared everything out. While she likely wouldn't find any information about Ian, she might dig up some other dirt on the organization.

Nylah hesitated. "Members of Mr. Butler's security detail were here earlier this afternoon and left with their things. They did not, however, have access to his room or yours, per your request."

"Are you sure they left the premises?"

Shaking her head, Nylah walked to her desk, opened a drawer then passed a master key card to Makenzie. "They departed about half an hour ago. They weren't here long."

Makenzie thanked Nylah and walked out the glass door with Ian. When they'd proceeded far enough to be out of earshot, she stopped, tapping the card against her palm.

"What's going through your head?" Ian's shoulder brushed hers as he scanned the terrain. A manicured lawn, dormant for the winter, rolled away from them down the mountain. Elegant white lights wove among the trees, shining in the late afternoon light. Foliage around the property was trimmed to perfection, casting long shadows as the sun edged lower in the sky.

Shadows that could hide a killer.

Cale and the rest of Butler's crew had better be long gone. "I'm debating if we should search the rooms or watch the footage first."

Ian stilled. "I'd like to see the footage."

The words were low, but Makenzie heard what he wasn't saying. "I don't know if it's a good idea for you to see what happened."

Surely there were cameras aimed at the outdoor patio on the parapet and along the arched walkway where she'd confronted Robert Butler as he'd dragged Ian away. She was curious, too, but allowing Ian to watch could be traumatic.

"It might help me remember, and it also might clue me in about who I was here to see. We can track my movements, see who I made contact with. The key might be right there."

It was possible the footage held a key, but would that key free Ian? Or lock him up forever?

Leaning against the wall by the door of the security office, Ian shoved his hands into his pockets and balled his fists. Far from the dimly lit high-tech control centers depicted in movies, the room was well-lit with a large desk in the center and a bank of monitors mounted like a mosaic on the wall before it.

Ian fought to keep from squirming. With his experience, he could run the machines better than the security guard manning them could.

He hated standing back. Not being in charge. Watching Makenzie do the work when *he* was the one in danger.

Watching Makenzie consistently walk into that danger in front of him.

It was only a matter of time before whoever was taking potshots at them landed a hit. They had to solve this. Soon. If Makenzie was hurt because of him...

He had a feeling it would be more devastating than he could currently imagine.

If the images he had flashed on were really memories, then they'd been closer than she was letting on.

He could ask, but he had a feeling she'd hedge the truth.

And he wasn't sure he was ready to know.

One thing he *did* know was that watching her in action as she took charge of the situation in the office had amped up his admiration for her. It also had made her about seven times more attractive than she already was.

She was tough. Capable.

She'd been his partner.

If only he could remember...

Ian glanced to where she leaned over the shoulder of a tech running video feeds. Was he really ready to see what those images would tell him about the previous night's events? Or about the person he couldn't remember becoming? No matter what he believed about who he was, he couldn't get around the facts.

He'd walked away from his team a year ago under shady circumstances.

He'd been at a wedding financed by an arms dealer.

He'd been marked for death by that same criminal because of his dealings with an *associate*.

None of this looked good. Not even to him.

Still, he couldn't imagine that kind of leap to the dark side. It wasn't in his nature.

So what had happened to change him in the past four years?

"Ian?"

Makenzie's voice pulled him from the spiraling darkness of his thoughts. She stood by the monitors, one hand braced on the table as she looked over her shoulder at him. "We've got you on arrival."

Pulling his hands from his pockets, he flexed his fingers and exhaled loudly, then fought a wince. All of those actions made him look weak. He might not know what he'd done for four years, but he was definitely a stronger man than he was behaving like at the moment.

It was time to face whatever he'd become.

As he walked over, Makenzie leaned down and spoke to the computer operator. The man hesitated, then stood and headed for the door, nodding to Ian as he passed. When he left, he shut the door quietly behind him.

"I bought us ten minutes." Makenzie settled into the chair and took the controls. "I'm pretty sure he wasn't supposed to leave us alone, but I didn't want him listening in. There's too much at stake."

Like his future.

While Ian really wanted to slide the controls away from her and take over, he kept his hands to himself. If they were going to add proof of his innocence to their arsenal of knowledge, then he couldn't touch the equipment. Anyone could argue he'd tampered with the footage.

Makenzie pointed to a screen, where an image was frozen.

It was him. He was handing his keys to a valet. He wore a slick navy blue suit, the kind he'd never choose for himself. It made him look like a James Bond wannabe. "Can that image be zoomed out? What kind of car was I driving? Is it still in the lot?"

Makenzie backed the feed up. The vehicle was a white Tesla Model S. High End. Electric. Even in his four-years-behind memory, the car had been top of the line, filled with the latest gadgets. It would even come when summoned with a cell phone, like a trusty horse.

The kind of thing a tech-savvy Bond villain might drive.

Swallowing hard, he eyed the vehicle.

"That car's way out of my price range." His voice was tight.

Makenzie offered no comment, simply pointed at the background. "That man in the shadows is Robert Butler. He's watching you from the moment you arrive. Something tipped him off. He told me someone was causing trouble for an associate, so he intended to take care of the problem. Unless we figure out who put him on your scent, we've got nothing."

How he wished he could remember.

They followed Ian from camera to camera, looping through different screens as he walked up the arched walkway and into the building. He spoke to various people along the way, but none more than casually. No objects passed between him and anyone else.

At one point, he walked within six feet of Makenzie, who stood with her back to him, watching the crowd.

The sight of her stopped his restless fidgeting. She was wearing the dressy pantsuit she'd had on at the hospital, but in the image it was much cleaner and had a flowing black jacket over it. Her hair was half up in some fancy hairstyle he didn't really understand, and she was wearing perfectly applied makeup.

She was drop-dead gorgeous. Like, walk-the-runway gorgeous.

He glanced down at her eyeing the screens, oblivious to his scrutiny. Somehow, he liked her better right now. No makeup. Hair hanging loose to her shoulders. It was…her. He didn't know how he knew what *her* was like, but he did.

She turned and caught him staring. "What?"

He forced a grin. "Wondering how long that supermodel look took to perfect."

She sniffed. "Too long." With a sigh, she turned to the screens. "I hated this op. Butler was the type who thought he was some sort of movie villain and wanted the whole hot female bodyguard thing. I've never missed jeans and sweatshirts so much in my life. I may never wear makeup again." Her eyebrows knit together as she ran the video forward then back again. She tapped the screen. "Watch your behavior here."

On the video, Ian turned. It was clear when he spotted Makenzie. His expression read as one of shock followed by a flicker of fear or concern. It was as though the sight of her froze his feet to the floor. One hand lifted as though he was going to reach out, but he suddenly turned and strode across the room, disappearing out the door to the parapet.

The outdoor camera picked him up. He walked nearly off-screen, braced his hands against the low stone wall and inhaled the night air so heavily that his shoulders heaved.

"Well, it's pretty clear I didn't expect to see you." He ran his hand over his mouth and down his chin. How should he interpret what his forgotten self was thinking?

Makenzie paused the screen on the image of his obvious discomfort. "No, and you weren't too happy about it either." Her tone implied he'd been afraid of getting caught.

He begged to differ. He might not remember what he was thinking, but he knew how he carried himself and how he reacted to fear, stress…sadness.

Walking closer to the table, he stood directly in front of the monitor and tried to insert himself into the scene. He hunched his shoulders to match his image's posture, trying to feel what he'd—

The memory of cold air slammed him. Cold air and cold stones. Even his insides shuddered.

Yes, he'd been terrified, but not for himself. The fear was for Makenzie.

Why?

He struggled to make the memory clearer, but it stuck on that one frame. The roadblock in his mind threatened to drag him into panic.

He breathed in for three beats…out for three beats. He could defeat this. He *had* to defeat this.

Without comment, Makenzie started the videos again. On the screen beside his image, the feed from inside the ballroom picked up Makenzie as she stood beside a display of Christmas trees. Rather than view his own turmoil, he watched as she studied the crowd with a practiced gaze. She didn't even flinch when Robert Butler approached from behind and stood a little too close. She turned down a glass of champagne which he held on to until after they had a tense conversation. Butler passed the glass to her and left the frame.

Makenzie paused the video and cleared her throat. "This is where he comes after you. Are you sure you want to watch?"

Ian nodded, but he was staring at the screen where Makenzie still held the glass of champagne. Something wasn't right.

It had everything to do with that glass. "Mak?"

She startled and looked up at him. It was almost as though the nickname had force. Maybe he used to call her that.

Not that the past mattered at the moment. He pointed at the screen. "Butler slammed his glass of champagne, but he never sipped the one he offered to you." He'd also handed it to her as he walked away. "Run back the video and follow him."

Makenzie's shoulders tensed, but she complied. If his hunch was right, then either the real target was Makenzie or someone knew exactly who both of them were and had attempted to literally kill two birds.

The images on all of the screens ran backward in a way that would have been comical at any other time. They followed Butler from one screen to another as he passed among camera angles.

Right to the moment when he poured a small vial into a glass of champagne.

Makenzie paused the image and stood, staring at the screen. "He knew." She dug her fist into the table. "How did he know? When did he know?"

Two more minutes of viewing told the tale. The outside cameras picked up Butler approaching a car a few minutes before Ian arrived, but the person in the back seat never got out. Instead, a brief conversation ensued in which Butler first looked confused, then angry. He watched Ian arrive then stalked inside and stood for a long time near the entrance, staring in Makenzie's direction with an angry glower before he flagged down the waiter for the champagne, then called one of his men over and directed the other man's attention to Makenzie.

Whatever was in that glass, he wanted someone to be watching when she went down.

Only she hadn't taken the bait.

Makenzie watched the feed two more times before she pounded her fist against the table, then jabbed her finger at the car on the screen, aiming at whoever Butler was speaking to. "That person. I want them. Because whoever is in that car tipped Butler off and wants both of us dead."

TEN

Makenzie had been ominously quiet since they'd discovered she was also a target.

As Ian trailed her out of the castle's administration building and into the valet parking lot down the hill, her silence crawled along his nerves.

He'd grown used to conversation as they'd both started to trust one another a little more. She bounced ideas off him, even though he could tell she stopped short of giving him every detail about the case.

Not that he could blame her, given his status with the team.

Everything was a discussion. Probably, during their partnership, there had been a lot of conversational give and take. It was likely they often went over the details of a case and laid theories out for one another's opinions.

He chewed the inside of his cheek. They'd probably worked well together. Like light squeezing around the edges of drawn curtains in his mind, he had the feeling they had. Not a single memory backed that up, but just like he'd known he'd been at her father's farm before, he knew they'd been a team the bad guys feared. "Maybe that's why someone is after us."

Makenzie stopped in the middle of the sidewalk, halfway between the building and the valet lot, and Ian stumbled to a stop to keep from running into her. "What?" She addressed the mountain that rose on the other side of the parking lot.

Ian stood beside her, careful not to touch her. If he did, he might get another mental image of a kiss. That was the last thing he needed right now. "Sorry. I was thinking out loud."

"You do that a lot. Well, you used to do that a lot." She continued to stare at the parking lot, where the white Tesla gleamed, alone in a sea of empty spaces. "I wonder why they haven't towed it?" She sniffed and turned her head to look at him. "So why do you think someone is after us?"

Her voice was tense in its too-calm timbre. She was angry and trying not to show it.

Thankfully, the anger wasn't directed at him this time. He inhaled deeply, trying to make the thought he hadn't meant to say out loud come together. It wasn't only his memory that was locked up. Butler's drug cocktail seemed to have slowed his creative mind, the part that let him conjecture about what a criminal might be thinking.

Or maybe he was just standing too close to Makenzie.

He eased away and shoved his hands into his pockets. "Okay. You and I were a team for how long?"

"Three years." Her voice was strung even tighter than it had been a few seconds earlier.

Probably because it bit her that he couldn't remember. He started to apologize, then opted not to. It wouldn't change the situation.

So he worked through his theory some more. "I'm guessing we made enemies. We probably put away a lot of powerful people who thought they were untouchable."

"We did." She gripped the Tesla's key fob, which she'd gotten from the office, tighter. "You know how Overwatch works. We investigate the investigators or the ones high enough to get wind of an Army Criminal Investigation Division inquiry. Or we go in where CID can't risk it because they're known. So, yeah. We brought down some big guns."

"Some who were law enforcement themselves."

"Yes?"

"*Military* law enforcement." He watched her, waiting for the light to come on.

When it did, she looked at him with the slightest upturn at the corners of her mouth. It wasn't joy. It was understanding. "Butler was stealing identities and arms from Southern military bases."

"Who would know the inner workings of a post better than someone who used to be in charge of guarding that very post? How to get around law enforcement? Who can be bribed? Where the weak spots are?"

"So you think someone we took down could have been in that car."

"Or someone who knew us when we were undercover recognized us." That was the more likely scenario. They needed to circle the fringes of their past investigations and see who might have let money turn their heads away from duty.

Well, Makenzie would have to. Obviously, he wasn't going to remember anything they'd worked on.

Her finger tapped the key fob, and she seemed to be reading the slope of the mountain. Suddenly, she frowned and shook her head. "Only problem is, I vetted the guest list myself. Anyone Butler didn't know personally, we ran a background check on. Of course, he didn't know I sent the entire list to Overwatch as well. There were no surprises. Not even you." She narrowed her eyes and turned, faced him fully. "Which begs the question… How did you slip past me and past Overwatch?"

"Alias?"

"You're good enough to hack yourself a new identity so, maybe." She started walking, faster this time, headed directly for the Tesla. "My laptop is upstairs. The guest list and the background checks are on it. We'll comb through it and see if we can find what name you used. I should have thought of that sooner." The recrimination in her voice was thick, but it didn't slow her pace.

If he was on the list at all, even with an alias. He could have come in under the radar. Ian rushed to catch up to her, noting the stiffness in her spine.

Makenzie slowed as she neared the vehicle and held her arm out to stop Ian's progress.

He halted just shy of her outstretched arm. "Do you see something?"

"No, but I've got two problems." She lowered her arm and cocked her head, eyeing the vehicle. "The first is easy. You can't go near that car."

Ian winced. No, he couldn't. Given that the unit suspected him of selling his hacking abilities to the bad guys, if he touched that vehicle it could lead to accusations of evidence tampering.

Makenzie was already dancing close to the line. She could already be accused of harboring a fugitive, given that she'd vanished with him and hadn't reached out to her chain of command. How was she going to get around that?

Hopefully, she had a plan. "What's the second problem?"

"If I wanted you dead, I'd wire your car."

That was also exactly what he'd do if he was on the wrong side of this. "Butler didn't have time between receiving his intel and coming after us."

"No, but clearly whoever ordered the hit knows you survived. They wouldn't have sent men to the hospital and the safe house otherwise." She shoved the key fob into his hand and walked toward the vehicle.

"I don't have the luxury of an explosives team. Stay here."

"Mak—" He bit down on the argument and wrapped his fingers around the key. What could he say? He couldn't touch the car. Couldn't even go near it.

Now that he held the key fob, that was doubly true. With proximity locks, if he got too close, the fob would ping the car to unlock the doors and...

He didn't want to consider what might happen next.

Makenzie strode across the pavement and crouched to look beneath the vehicle as best she could given its low ground clearance. The car was made for speed, not for off-roading. It would be tough to see underneath without proper equipment.

Hopefully, whoever was targeting them had stayed away from the vehicle. Given that it was in valet parking, a civilian could have been at risk. That might be enough to stop some killers, but if they were ruthless enough, collateral damage wouldn't matter.

Ian's muscles didn't relax until Makenzie had made a full circle of the car and stood, swiping her hands together. "I don't see anything out of place." She rounded the vehicle to the side closest to him. "Stay where you are and toss me the fob."

No way. If she was going to blow up when that thing got into range, he was going with her. Whether he remembered her or not, she was his partner. They walked this road together.

She glared at him as he walked toward her. "Ian, this is—"

The door locks popped.

They both jumped.

The vehicle didn't explode.

Willing his heart to beat again, Ian plopped the fob into her outstretched hand. The security cameras were watching and could be used against both of them if he dared to get any closer.

Makenzie donned the latex gloves she'd obtained from housekeeping and searched the vehicle. His fingers clenched and opened, over and over. This was about him. What had he left behind in that car? Could

this prove his innocence? Or would it con-
demn him?

It was all he could do not to rock from
heel to toe like a toddler in time-out.

Finally, years after she started, Makenzie slammed the trunk and stripped off the
gloves, shoving them into her pockets with
a scowl.

She was frustrated and empty-handed.

He met her halfway. "What?"

"There's nothing there."

Should he be relieved or disappointed?
"No registration? No papers?"

"Not even a chewing gum wrapper in
the cup holder. That car's hasn't been this
empty since it rolled off the assembly line."
She dragged her hand through her hair and
looked over her shoulder at the vehicle.
"Even the owner's manual is missing. I'm
guessing if we had the ability to run the
VIN, it would come up stolen. The plates
are fake. Good forgeries, but still fake."

"Give me a computer." He could hack the
state's database and run the VIN in about
ten seconds. He could also search stolen

vehicle reports, which could give them an idea of where he'd obtained the vehicle.

"No." Her voice was firm, brooking no argument. Without looking at him, she stepped around him and stalked toward the building.

Ian watched her walk away, his hands dropping to his sides.

She still didn't trust him. Might never trust him.

At this moment, he wasn't even certain he trusted himself.

The spiral staircase shook slightly as Makenzie ascended toward her guest room, her footsteps echoing off of the castle's medieval atrium. Anger coursed through her, hot and volatile.

She'd needed a moment, some time to cool off and think straight before they moved forward.

Ian was in the control room with two security guards, searching for a way to identify who was in that vehicle. The system ran on a closed circuit, so he had no access to the internet, and two guards who were former Special Forces who, at her request, wouldn't let him get far if he managed to slip away.

She hated her suspicions of the man she'd once trusted without question. It had taken time for him to earn that trust, given her history.

He'd crushed it in a day.

In a perfect world, there would have been evidence of Ian's innocence in that car. Evidence that provided a reason for his disappearance and subsequent silence.

The pain on his face when she'd told him *no* had just about brought her to her knees. A wiped clean, possibly stolen car had shaken her fragile trust in him. *God, I need proof he's innocent. Please.*

Nothing fell out of the sky so she kept stalking up the stairs, her footfalls echoing a new refrain. *Someone. Blew. My. Cover.*

The key was the person in that car. They were likely who Butler was supposed to meet, possibly Storm. They'd also recognized both Ian and Makenzie and had known they were both present at the reception.

She had a strong feeling the person might be able to provide clues to where Ian had been for the past year.

At the door to Butler's room, she forced her thoughts on to task, drew her weapon and slipped inside. She cleared the room and flipped the door lock into place before she holstered her Sig and headed for the sofa. Pulling the left cushion from its place, she unzipped it and retrieved the eleven-inch laptop that Butler had received from Storm only days before. She grabbed his main laptop as well, a larger model that he tended to use as a showpiece, too unwieldy to be of any real use.

She smirked. He'd typically used the machine to play online games and watch videos. Most of his money trail was on the laptop she used. If he was ever caught, he likely intended to make her his fall guy.

Too bad for him that he didn't realize she was the hunter he'd hoped to evade.

Bristling with fresh anger, she slipped out

the door, scanned the area then swiped into her room across the hall. He'd wanted adjoining rooms, but she'd insisted on being out of reach.

Good thing, too, since he'd tried to poison her.

In the room she shut the door and leaned against it, hugging the laptops to her chest. For a couple of days, this room had been the only place where she could be Makenzie Fuller instead of Mack Fullerton. She'd been able to shed the undercover role and relax.

No time for that now, although she'd love to grab her comfy pj's from the drawer and hug them close. She'd never even gotten to soak in the massive Jacuzzi tub.

Quickly, Makenzie shoved the laptops into her suitcase along with her computer, tablet and e-reader. She tossed in clothes as well. Satisfied she'd retrieved everything of value, she peered out the peephole then opened the door and wheeled her luggage into the hall.

Someone grabbed her arm, twisted it behind her and shoved her into the doorframe face-first. Her cheek crashed painfully into metal. The suitcase slipped from her grasp.

A force pressed against her back, smashing her face harder into the cold frame. "I knew you'd be here."

Cale Nicholson.

Stupid. She should have kept her guard up. Shouldn't have let anger and frustration rush her. The smart move would have been to run today's security feed to make sure Butler's men had left the premises before she started traipsing around.

Shifting, she tried to get her leg high enough to drive her heel into his instep, but he had her pinned too tightly.

Her elbow would have to do the trick.

Before she could fight, something hard pressed into her side, drawing a gasp.

Cale leaned closer, his breath hot on her ear. "You're alive because you know the password to Butler's computer, but I'll put a bullet in you and find a hacker if I need to." He forced the pistol deeper between her ribs, and the pain drew tears. "Actually, that might not be the worst idea I've had today. I've waited too long to knock you down a few pegs already."

Wait. Not a word about her being undercover. Although the video made it appear he'd asked Nicholson to watch her, it seemed as though he hadn't passed along the reason why.

She might have a fighting chance. "Back off, Cale. I know more about how to run this organization than you do. You kill me and you'll have to rebuild from the ground up. There won't be many buyers with the patience to wait on you to figure it all out." She laughed, forcing herself into the bitter, world-weary front she'd worn around the men. "You'll lose everything."

Every muscle in his body tensed. The war between what she was saying and what he wanted to do to her was almost audible. The gun dug deeper into her side.

Suddenly, he shoved the center of her back and stepped away.

Makenzie exhaled. It had worked.

When she turned, he pressed the gun

Blown Cover

tight to her forehead, backing her against the wall.

Although her heart hammered that this could be the last minute of her life, she rolled her eyes. "Don't be an idiot. No hacker on the planet will work with you if it gets out that you offed Butler's number two. If we join forces, you can kill me later."

"I'm not stupid. You'll kill me first." He held out his hand. "Laptop. Password." He grinned. "Boom."

She'd shake her head if she could move. This guy was a bigger rookie than he realized if he was talking like a movie villain. "Here's how I know you're going to fail, Nicholson."

"Yeah?"

"Yeah." She raised an eyebrow. "You put your gun in easy reach." Throwing her hand up sharply, she knocked his arm to the side.

The weapon fired into the wall beside her head, the crack of the shot ringing her ears and echoing in her skull.

Tipping her shoulder, she leveraged off the door, driving Cale backward into the wall. His head thudded against the rough stone. He grunted as his gun clattered to the floor.

He fought with a vengeance driven by pain. His fist connected with Makenzie's stomach, forcing the air from her lungs.

It was just enough for him to slide past her.

As he reached for her suitcase while on the run, he stumbled.

Makenzie dove, taking him out at the knees.

He face-planted to the cobblestone floor. She clawed her way onto his back and drew her Sig, pressing the barrel to the base of his skull. There was no way he could reach her weapon the way she had him pinned. Unlike him, she knew better. "I dare you to move." Normally, she wouldn't threaten his life, but her persona demanded it.

Breathing heavily, Nicholson let loose a string of curses that should have withered

Makenzie from the inside out. It would feel so good to announce her true identity and arrest him, but she wanted answers.

She pressed the barrel tighter against his skull. "Question. What did Butler say to you about me? At the reception?"

"He'd hit your drink with one of his magic concoctions." His chuckle was almost slimy. "He was tired of waiting on you to warm up. Wanted me to deliver you to his room."

She tried not to shudder, although she doubted it was true. Butler relied on his prowess with women. Prided himself in it. More likely he'd used her constant refusals as a cover for his colossal mistake in trusting an undercover agent. Given the rumblings against her in the organization, he'd never want his men to know how royally he'd messed up.

What had he said about Ian? "Who was the guy that Butler wanted dead?"

"The one you snuck out of the hospital with?" He spit the words against the stone floor.

No mention of the safe house. *Interesting.* "Maybe I need to take care of that problem."

"Forget it."

"Tell me or I finish what you tried to start." She hated the threat, but the only thing Nicholson cared about was himself.

He cursed again. "You know more than me. Butler said the guy was trying to double-cross Storm."

So all of this truly did circle back to Storm.

Footsteps pounded up the hallway.

Makenzie glanced over her shoulder.

Ian stopped several feet away with three armed security guards. She gave him a hard look, tipping her head toward the stairwell. *Get out of sight.*

With a nod, he spoke to the security guard nearest him, then disappeared through the stairwell door.

From her discussions with the staff when Butler was booking the castle, she knew these guys were former military. They'd know how to handle the situation.

One of the guards acknowledged her with a professional nod, then raised his voice. "Drop your weapon."

Makenzie almost grinned. Ian had taken steps to protect her cover. While someone knew her identity, Butler's men seemed to be in the dark. The last thing she needed was Nicholson singing from a prison cell about her status as an undercover agent. Her life would never be her own.

Muttering beneath her breath, she laid the gun out of Nicholson's reach and let the security guard drag her to her feet. He retrieved her gun and escorted her up the hall as the other two men took Nicholson into custody.

In the stairwell, he returned her weapon and she briefed him on who Cale Nicholson was. She also gave him Tangaro's number. This was a way to check in without directly making contact if someone truly had double-crossed them. "Tell them I'm safe and still investigating. I'll reach out when I can." That should be enough to cover her without giving away where they were staying.

She didn't mention Ian. That was a bridge she'd cross later.

As the guard tapped notes into his phone, Ian eyed her with concern.

Makenzie ignored him.

The guard finished. "They're taking him down the back stairway and we'll tell him we're keeping you separated as a precaution. Anything else?"

"I need my suitcase." No way was she handing Butler's devices over until she'd investigated them. Those machines could reveal the identity of the person who wanted them dead. With a possible mole on the team, she couldn't risk evidence disappearing.

The guard ducked through the door, and Makenzie turned to Ian.

His blue eyes were an ocean storm. "I saw what happened on the security cameras. We got here as fast as we could."

"I had it covered."

"I noticed." He swallowed so hard she could hear it. "What's next?"

"We need to find out who was in that car."

They had to do it quickly, too. Because if a traitor had infiltrated Overwatch, then the danger would only grow deadlier.

ELEVEN

Makenzie dropped onto the bench in the downstairs mudroom and slumped against the wall as Zane continued past her up the stairs to check on Noah. It had been dark by the time they made it to Asheville, dropped off the rental car and met her brother for a ride to the farm.

She was pretty sure they'd avoided security cameras and tails, but nothing was ever certain.

Beside her, Ian mimicked her posture, stretching his legs in front of him. "You're sure about staying here?"

Did she have a choice? They needed to be where help was available. Where someone with training could watch their backs.

Until they knew who they could trust, she couldn't reveal their location to anyone in the unit. While trust had never come easily, she'd never expected to be in a position where everyone in Eagle Overwatch was suspect.

Where she'd have to rely on the man who'd shattered what remained of her trust. She hadn't considered what she'd do when she stepped out of Mack Fullerton's shoes and into Makenzie Fuller's again. Being cynical and suspicious was part of the undercover job. But on the outside? It made for a miserable way of life. She'd buried her feelings about Ian during the op.

Now she was being forced to confront them head-on in the most literal way.

"Mak?" Ian tapped her toe with his. "You hear me?"

She tried to ignore how that tiny contact swirled her stomach. She wanted to believe him. Needed to trust him. Had to battle each moment with herself to remain vigilant and suspicious.

It was exhausting. She sighed. "Given that whoever is hunting us knows me, they could find us here, so I'm not totally sure.

However, there's nowhere safer." All of her father's security measures would protect them from any assault.

"Think you'll be able to sleep?"

Makenzie smiled wearily. "No." Especially not with her fingers itching to open Butler's laptops. Problem was, she'd need a hacker to get into the one Storm had given to Butler. Someone with the kind of skills Ian possessed.

As much as she longed to trust him, twenty-four hours wasn't enough time to erase a year of silence and circumstantial evidence.

After kicking off her shoes, Makenzie grabbed her suitcase and climbed the stairs with Ian close behind.

Her father waited in the kitchen with sandwiches, coffee and tea. His hug engulfed Makenzie, swallowing her in a familiarity that kicked her to the months after her mother's death. To the weeks after Coach Davies was arrested and her lies shredded Makenzie's faith.

"Little girl, you can't scare me like that."

She'd briefed her father on Nicholson's arrest when she'd called to let him know they were headed back from the castle.

"It's my job, Dad." She pulled away and ran her hands down the front of her shirt, trying to force her emotions into hiding. "It sounds worse than it actually was. I had everything under control."

Her dad looked at Ian. "Did she?"

"She did." The way Ian watched her, with admiration plainly written on his face...

The flames in her cheeks felt real, and they fired straight from the heat in her heart.

Ducking her head, Makenzie grabbed the suitcase handle and rolled it into the corner on the far side of the kitchen table. It gave her a chance to get her nervous system into line with her head and to move the laptops out of Ian's reach. On the off chance he was playing her, she needed to keep them close.

When she sat at the table, his eyes clouded and he looked away. No doubt he knew what she was thinking.

She hated herself for it.

He backed toward the door. "I'm going to get some sleep." Without even a nod, he disappeared around the corner, his footfalls heavy on the stairs.

She couldn't blame him. It was the second time today her actions had called him a criminal.

As an investigator, she couldn't take a chance. She had to maintain the chain of custody. Letting Ian near those laptops could be used against them later, whether he was innocent or not.

When her father slipped into the chair beside hers, shoving a sandwich and hot tea her way, she wrapped her fingers around the mug. Her stomach was in no mood for food. "Where's Noah?" He was at the forefront of her thinking. Having him here while she was in danger made her question everything.

"He racked out hours ago. Zane had him out in the yard playing soccer all afternoon."

Makenzie reached for a sandwich and tore the crust off. "How's he doing on his rec team?" Noah had always wanted to play soccer *just like Aunt Mak.*

Zane never should have told him that she used to play, that she'd been good enough to be a pro. Too much pain permeated that season of her life.

"Turns out, he's a natural as a goalie, just like you." Her dad chuckled, but the mirth didn't reach his eyes. They never discussed her time on the field. "First time they put him in the net, he stopped everything that came at him, even though he's one of the youngest on the team." He took a sip of coffee. "Maybe Aunt Mak can give him some pointers."

"Aunt Mak hasn't touched a soccer ball since college." Not even for Noah. It hurt too much to think of what might have been if her coach hadn't been arrested for recruitment violations and embezzlement and the program dismantled.

Her dad shrugged. "I hate to see you let go of something you loved."

"Well, there've been a lot of things I've loved and lost, so I've had practice." Her mother… soccer… Audra… Ian… "The list gets longer every day."

"It's all in your face right now, isn't it?" Between her father and Zane, growing up in the Fuller house had been like living with two mind readers. They all knew each other that well.

"The whole ride home, I kept thinking about Audra. She'd have closed this case already. Here I am, with this Storm person outing me and endangering our lives…" She was a failure.

Her father shoved his coffee mug across the table and sat back, crossing his arms over his stomach. "I remember how hard her death hit you."

Makenzie's throat ached with rising tears. She'd been one of the first on the scene when Audra was located. India Garrison's henchmen had been thorough in their work. The arms dealer had made certain there was little of Audra left to identify, but dental records had told the awful tale.

Regret was a beast, and it reared its ugly head. Audra had told Makenzie she thought someone was stalking her. It would have been so easy to back her up. When she was snatched out of the parking lot at the grocery store, the entire Portland office had galvanized to find her. They were too late. "I miss her every day."

"I know." He finally met her gaze. "You still idolize her."

"How could I not?" Audra had been a flawless agent and an even better friend. "Everything I know in this job I learned from her. Even how to square my shoulders and be a woman in a man's world."

"Audra was human. She wasn't perfect. Sometimes I get the feeling you think she was."

Makenzie glanced away, watching the door that led to the living room. Ian had said that to her before as well. So had Major Tangaro. And others.

"How did Ian measure up?" This time, when her dad sipped his coffee, he watched her over the rim of the cup with an amused expression.

Tears pressed behind her eyes. Maybe

it was because they were talking about Audra.

Or maybe it was because she still felt the same emotions she always had for Ian. The ones he'd crushed under his heel when he disappeared. The ones she'd buried while undercover. The ones that were bruised every time she remembered he had no memory of their past, no matter how familiar he acted.

"You still love him?"

Sniffing, Makenzie pressed her fingertips to her eyes. She was exhausted, emotionally charged and chasing an adrenaline crash. If she wasn't careful, she'd melt into a heap of overwrought tears.

Her dad had always been a good listener. So many nights, she'd sat at this very kitchen table and puzzled out the stomach-churning twists of life. "I don't know." The words muffled into her palms.

"What don't you know?"

"You were an officer in the CIA, Dad. You know how this works." She dropped her hands to the table and traced the rim of her tea glass. "He's suspected of some pretty treacherous stuff."

"Never proven."

"Now he has amnesia, which is convenient given he showed up at a wedding thrown by an arms dealer on the same night a serious merger was in the works."

"So, you don't believe him?"

"I do. Mostly. He hasn't slipped once. Either way, he doesn't remember anything about me other than a few watercooler conversations right after I transferred. It's like—" The tears almost forced their way out. She cleared her throat and tried again. "Like I never existed. Like *we* never existed. He doesn't look at me the way he used to. Doesn't talk to me the way he used to."

"That's why I buy that he has amnesia. No man is that good of a liar." He sat forward and rested his warm hand on her wrist. "He was very serious before."

She sniffed. "How do you know?"

His gaze skittered to the side. "I just do."

That wasn't the whole truth. Her father had a tell.

So did Ian. It crept in whenever he was in undercover mode, not acting as himself. It was a tic at the corner of his eye, as though his body betrayed the truth.

Never once had she seen that tell when he was talking to her, not even the day before he vanished. "It's funny but the guy he is today is the guy he was all along...other than being in love with me." She winced. The L-word had never actually come up between them, but she couldn't deny she'd once felt it.

"Do you remember your mother's partner at the law firm?"

Guess her dad was tired of talking about her, but the path of the conversation was definitely twisty. "Elias?"

"Elias MacIntosh." Her father practically spit the name. "He was arrogant. He had a thing for your mother."

Makenzie's head jerked. Her father had never sung Elias's praises, but this was news.

"They worked closely with one another and, at first, it made me a little jealous. You know how it goes. Long days. Long nights. Especially when a big case was in the works. My head used to make me think the craziest things."

She genuinely couldn't imagine, especially since her parents had been so close. "How did you handle it?"

"I decided I knew my wife well, and I made the choice to trust her and who I knew her to be. Otherwise, we had no basis for a marriage." He clasped his hands on the table. "You say Ian seems to be the same guy he always was. If that's the case, then you have a choice to make. Either you trust him or you don't. If you don't? Then his innocence or guilt doesn't matter, because you have no foundation for a partnership or a relationship."

Maybe he should leave.

Ian rolled over and punched the pillow on the bed he hadn't bothered to crawl into. Too exhausted to care, he'd dropped on the quilt and fallen asleep before he could acknowledge the bitterness in his gut.

The burn of it woke him at dawn.

Makenzie still didn't trust him.

Should it matter what a stranger thought of him anyway?

At least…to him she was a stranger. To her, they'd been teammates and, he was convinced, something more.

All he had was the vague notion he'd been to this house before, the flash of a kiss and the image of himself on a screen, frightened for Makenzie.

Seeing her with a gun pressed to the base of her skull…

That last one almost made him want to curl into the fetal position. He couldn't let himself go to what could have happened, not if he wanted to fix things now.

As morning outlined objects in the small bedroom, he flopped onto his back and stared at the ceiling. If he could slip away, maybe whoever was tailing them would come after him and leave her alone.

Although she was a target as well.

Fleeing would only make him look guilty, and it would leave her even more vulnerable.

Besides, if he left now, he might never know what Makenzie was hiding from him. His brain might not recollect, but his chest kept beating that their relationship had been deeper than she let on. If he could put the pieces together...

There were no pieces though. Just a giant gap in his memories, threatening to swallow his identity whole.

A raging wave of anxiety drove him from the bed and sent him pacing between the door and the window. Fear bubbled in his veins. He balled his fists, trying to find a pinpoint of light, some truth of who he'd become floating in that black hole.

Only darkness loomed.

He wanted to put his fist into the wall. Anything to jar a memory. Instead he closed his eyes and pressed his forehead against the window frame, relishing the cool pressure. Maybe it would open a valve. *Lord, bring it back.*

"Ian?" Makenzie's low voice spun him on his heel.

She stood in the doorway, uncertain and

nervous. Her hair was somehow different, probably because she'd washed it. An oversize hunter green sweater hung to her jean-covered thighs.

She'd cleaned up and changed clothes, but had she slept?

Wrestling his emotions into check, he stared at her, the one thing that tied his past to his present. "You okay?"

Tilting her head to the side, she watched him, her right hand fiddling with the hem of her sweater.

At one time, he'd apparently been good at knowing her thoughts. If only he'd retained that talent.

Finally, her fingers stopped worrying her sweater. "Can you meet me in the kitchen after you get a shower?" She turned and left him alone.

Something beyond their circumstances was bothering her. If he could remember anything, maybe he'd know what it was.

He took a quick shower, brushed his teeth, changed into clothes borrowed from her brother and headed up the stairs to the living area.

A child's laugh bounced toward him from the kitchen. Ian followed the sound and found Zane settling a plate of eggs in front of Noah.

Makenzie was nowhere to be seen.

Zane looked up as he turned away from the table. "Morning, Ian."

Shoving in a mouthful of eggs he'd dragged through a mound of ketchup, Noah offered a wave before he turned his attention fully to the plate in front of him.

"Can't wait to see how he eats as a teenager." Zane chuckled. "You hungry? There's eggs and bacon."

While the bacon smelled almost as tempting as the chili had the day before, Ian shook his head. What he really wanted was to find Makenzie.

As if he could read Ian's mind, Zane headed to the stove with his pan, tilting his head toward the living room behind Ian. "She went to Dad's office on the other side of the house."

"Thanks." It was probably rude to refuse breakfast, and his stomach would revolt if he didn't eat soon, but he was driven to find her, drawn to what the parts of him that couldn't remember somehow instinctively knew.

He was also desperate to find his way into her trust. Somehow he knew she'd been important to him.

Who was he kidding? She was important to him now. He might not remember her with his mind, but he sure did remember her with his heart. The jolt of her in danger yesterday solidified it.

She was special. He just couldn't put into words how he knew that.

Other than he couldn't stop replaying what had happened on the deck. Or the image of a kiss that kept looping into his brain.

He wouldn't mind creating a new version of that memory.

James Fuller's office was more of a dark-paneled library with floor-to-ceiling bookshelves on one wall. High windows

overlooked the property as it rolled away
to the mountains. In the center of the room,
in front of the bookcase wall, Makenzie sat
at a large glass desk facing the door. Two
laptops sat open in front of her, and she was
focused on the larger one.

She didn't seem to notice he'd stopped in
the doorway.

For a moment, Ian watched her work.
She was absorbed in her reading, absently
running her finger along the edge of the
laptop's trackpad. The unguarded moment
found its way into his heart and snagged
on a vague memory that drew him to her.

As though she could hear his thoughts,
she looked up and motioned for him to
enter. Pointing to a kitchen chair she'd set
in front of the second laptop, she held his
gaze. "I need your help."

Was she saying what he thought she was?
Adrenaline hit his system. She was going
to give him a crack at that laptop. Let him
do his job.

She was choosing to trust him.

It brought an odd feeling to the back of

his throat, tightening his vocal cords so that it took a moment to speak. "Are you sure?"

Without hesitation, she nodded. "Ian, I don't know what happened. I don't know why you left or who you became, but I know who you were when you were my partner. I know who you are right now. You're the only person in my current circle who can get into that laptop and possibly figure out who's after us, maybe even find the mole in our unit. I'm pretty sure the answer lies with Storm, and he handed Butler that laptop."

"His newest business partner." Ian pulled the chair out and slid into it, hands on the keyboard before he was even fully seated.

He pulled them back before he started. This was thin ice. He could work on the laptop, but only under Makenzie's strict supervision. He had to be careful not to make one wrong move, or any evidence would be considered compromised.

First, he had to get in. "Did Butler set the password or did Storm?"

"It was set before Butler received it. I can

tell you a whole lot about Butler, but none of it is going to help you guess a password he didn't come up with himself." She slid an external drive across the small space between them, leaving her hand on the device. "This is a drive you prepped before this mission. It's your software. You always said it was a master key to any system."

Ian stared at her hand over the small rectangular hard drive. She was literally handing him the keys to the kingdom.

He remembered that software. At least, he remembered when he was developing it. The program was a next-gen password cracker.

Over the past few years, he'd obviously perfected it or come close. If he'd managed to get it to work the way he'd planned, then Makenzie was handing him a tool that would allow him to hack into almost any system, even ones run by the government.

It would definitely crack any personal laptop out there.

Given that his team suspected he'd sold his skills to the dark side, this was huge.

He couldn't take his eyes off what this represented. When he reached for the drive, slowly, Makenzie didn't pull her hand away. Laying his hand over hers, he curled his fingers around her warm, slender ones. He couldn't look at her. Couldn't breathe. If he did, his heart might start saying things that his head didn't understand. "Thank you."

Gently, she pulled her hand from his and started typing on her laptop. "I kept my data in a secure cloud server. I sent copies to the unit for analysis and kept a separate set of data on my own server so I could access it without drawing suspicion from anyone on Butler's team. No one should be able to track me since no one knows about it. I'm going to see what I can dig up."

Ian merely nodded, then plugged in the drive and paused with his hand over the smaller laptop. His brain was spinning, playing with worst-case scenarios. "We need to think this through. If I was Storm's people and I was setting up this laptop, then I'd put in a tracker that would kick in any time it powered on or hooked up to Wi-Fi."

"I was afraid of that."

"There's one thing…" Man, feeling useful was a rush. "One of the first things I did when I started work on this software was develop a location blocker that kicks in the instant the computer is turned on. It might ping, but only for a millisecond, not long enough to be tracked." He glanced at her. "Are you willing to take the risk I got that working?"

"You used to talk geek-speak to me a lot. I vaguely remember you being very excited about blocking locations."

"Hmm." If he had, then he was pretty much a rock star. "I hope you're remembering right."

"We don't have a choice, do we?"

"Not if we want answers." Ian pressed the power button and the machine fired up, immediately asking for a password. Beside him, the drive whirred.

"Just make sure your head doesn't inflate so much that it can't get out the door. I know how you think."

"Copy that." He fought the urge to crack his knuckles. She knew him well, even if he didn't remember. "I'll try to remain humble." Although it felt good to be working in his wheelhouse, being productive.

Except, for him, technology was four years ahead of his remembered skill set. Technology changed quickly. What if he couldn't control his own software? What if he couldn't crack this password?

Pulling up a command window, he poised his fingers over the keyboard and stared at the blinking cursor.

His thoughts mushed into alphabet soup. Knitting his eyebrows together, he tried to force a memory of how this worked.

The rising panic that had ebbed in the bedroom rushed back in a tidal wave. His hands shook. His heart pounded. His thoughts fell over the edge into the dark abyss.

He had to get out of here.

Slamming the laptop shut, he shoved the

chair away from the desk and bolted from
the room, desperate for air.

Desperate for freedom.

TWELVE

On the patio, the air was damp and cold, holding the scent of approaching snow. Ian inhaled more and more of it, trying to fill his lungs, praying the chill would flush the heat from his rushing blood.

He couldn't think. Couldn't process.

Whatever drug Robert Butler had forced into his system, it had stolen his memories and his talents. He wasn't himself. Might never be again.

Panic slammed him in the chest. *Fight or flight*.

He chose *flight*.

Ian let go, allowing the energy in his body to release the way it had begged to ever since he'd awakened, helpless in a hospital bed. The pressure exploded as he ran, racing across the yard toward the barns at the bottom of the hill, squinting against the glare of winter clouds. He had no idea where he was going. No clue what he'd do when he got there.

If he ran fast enough, maybe he'd catch up to his memories and to who he really was.

When he reached the barn, his energy crashed. It was like someone had opened a dam and the lake gushed out. Empty. Whatever had wreaked havoc on his mind still hadn't let go of his body either.

While he was bending at the waist, his temple brushed a vine that grew up the side of the barn. He braced his hands on his knees and tried to pray.

No words would come. Even the faith part of him seemed to have succumbed to the drug. He was completely lost.

"What are you doing out here?" Noah's voice broke through the pounding in his ears.

Ian jerked upright. Noah stood behind the barn about ten feet away, holding a soccer ball. On the other side of the small barnyard, a soccer goal held court, waiting for a shot.

Exhaling through pursed lips, Ian tried to slow his heart rate and his raging thoughts. He couldn't scare Makenzie's nephew by tearing around like a wild animal. The kid had enough going on with his mom being gone for Christmas. He didn't need a stranger bringing panic and danger.

Lord, coming here was a bad idea, wasn't it? No matter what Makenzie said about the safety of the farm, he had to wonder if it was truly okay for Noah to be present. He turned his eyes to the sky, managing to utter a prayer for safety and to catch his breath before he tipped his chin down to look at the little boy.

Tossing the soccer ball lightly, Noah watched him with a practiced eye. "Is something chasing you?"

Only my nightmares. "Nope. Thought I'd go for a run." It wasn't a lie, given the way his mind had driven his entire person into motion. "Where's your dad?"

"Over there. He got a phone call. Again." Noah's eye roll was a little too adult.

Ian bit back a smile and followed the direction Noah pointed.

At the far side of the barnyard, near the edge of the apple orchard, Zane paced, phone pressed to his ear. He nodded a greeting when Ian caught his eye, then returned to his conversation.

Wonder what that was about.

"So did you come out here looking for Santa? It's too soon for him to be on the way."

Just like that, the kindergartner returned.

Grateful for distraction, Ian followed him down the conversational rabbit trail. "Plus it's daylight."

"Dad said he heard sleigh bells out here and we should come look."

Smart guy, that Zane. He'd likely distracted Noah to get him out of the house while Makenzie and Ian were working.

Or *not* working, in his case.

Crouching on one knee, Ian got down to Noah's eye level. "He could be checking out his route one more time, making sure he knows where he's going so there are no surprises on the big night."

"Or he sent one of the elves to do it?" Green eyes lit with Christmas magic.

Oh, to be that innocent again. "I'm sure that's it. So how many days until Christmas? I bet you know exactly."

"Four sleeps. After the third sleep is Christmas Eve, so that one really doesn't count."

"Smart kid. You're right." He tapped the soccer ball Noah held. It had obviously been kicked around quite a bit. "Did you ask Santa for a new ball?"

"I don't want a new ball."

"Really? Looks like this one is ready to retire."

"Nope. Aunt Mak gave this to me when I was born. It's special." He hugged the ball to his chest in the same way most kids would snuggle a puppy.

Ian glanced toward the house, out of sight on the other side of the barn. He'd have to face Makenzie eventually, but not now. The humiliation was too great. The stakes were too high.

He was no help.

"Talking about soccer?" Zane walked over and dropped to the ground beside Ian, resting his elbows on his bent knees.

"And the ball Aunt Mak gave me when I was born." Noah likely didn't see Makenzie often, but clearly Zane and his wife had done a good job of keeping her memory fresh. Noah clearly loved her, and he spoke about her with adoration.

Well, Ian certainly couldn't blame the kid for that one.

Zane settled his phone on the ground between his feet. "Did Noah tell you he's a soccer prodigy?"

"What's a projidy?" He tripped over the word, then looked at his dad for help.

"A *prodigy*. It's someone who's good at something without trying. It's like you're born knowing how to do it. Like you as a goalie."

Noah's head bobbed up and down. "Yeah.

That's me. I'm a goalie projidy. At least, I am sometimes."

"Sometimes?" Zane tapped Noah's nose with his index finger and turned to Ian with the proudest dad look imaginable. "My kid rocks the goal. Nothing gets past him."

"Daddy says I have Aunt Mak's genes." Noah sat on the ground, mimicking his father's posture. He squeezed the soccer ball between his knees. "She was really good."

She was? "Makenzie played soccer?"

"I keep forgetting you don't remember things." Zane stared over Ian's shoulder. "She was professional-level good."

Of all the things he'd have guessed about Makenzie, soccer phenom wasn't on the list. "What happened?"

Lips pressed tightly together, Zane shook his head. "That's her story to tell."

"I probably already know it." Like so many other things.

"You definitely do." The pity in Zane's expression was more than Ian could take.

He turned away, focusing on Noah and

his innocence. "So goalie is your thing, huh?"

"When I'm not thinking."

Zane chuckled.

"Okay." Ian dragged the word out. "What does that mean?"

Clearly done with sitting still, Noah rocketed to his feet and dribbled the soccer ball, kicking it gently in a circle around his father and Ian. "I just do better when I don't think. When I just play."

"That's true." Zane leaned over and punched the soccer ball sideways.

Noah chased it, laughing as he caught up to the ball and charged the goal with it.

Zane watched then picked up his phone again, turning it over in his hands. "I'm taking Noah to my sister-in-law's house." He watched the device, not looking at Ian.

It was a smart idea, getting the kid away from danger.

Problem was, Ian was the danger. "I'm sorry."

"For what?"

A thousand things he couldn't remember. "You guys had Christmas planned, and now Makenzie and I—"

"Don't." Zane leaned sideways, shoving his phone into his pocket. "Noah loves his cousins. He'll have a blast there. If you guys think you need me, I'll come back for a few days then leave Christmas Eve morning." He held up a hand. "Don't argue. Right now, getting you and Mack through this is a bigger priority. You need me and Dad."

"Noah needs you."

Zane started to speak, but the soccer ball whacked his arm and Noah raced up behind it. "You were supposed to block it."

"Well, I didn't see it coming." Zane's laugh was forced.

Hopefully, Noah wouldn't notice.

Ian cast around for something to say to ease the tension that hung amidst the three of them. "So you play better when you don't think?"

"Yeah, when I just be."

Ian arched an eyebrow.

"The word you're looking for is *over-*

think." Zane chuckled. "Noah is unstoppable when he quits thinking about how to play. He's like his mother. He tends to think too much about what might happen. To analyze every move. Goalie is a quick-reaction position. When he gets out of his head? He's a beast."

Overthinking. Ian's jaw slacked. Every time he tried to force a memory or an action, his brain fogged and his body froze.

Maybe Zane and Noah were onto something. He shoved to his feet. "I'm going for a walk." And some prayer. He ruffled Noah's hair as he passed and shot a confused-looking Zane a grateful smile before he headed for the rows of trees at the edge of the apple orchard. Peace was there. It had to be.

If he'd quiet his mind enough that he might find some answers.

Somewhere in the orchard, Ian was wandering alone.

Lifting her foot from the gas pedal on the farm truck, Makenzie turned down "I'll

Be Home for Christmas" and scanned the aisles between the trees. The morning sun cast milky light through thickening clouds. It did little to warm December air laced with the scent of Christmas from the fir trees on the other side of the orchard.

She'd almost followed Ian out of the house, but when she'd spotted him talking to Noah and Zane, she'd backed off. Let him have some guy time.

When they returned to the house, he wasn't with them.

No way would she let him walk this road alone.

While Ian might not remember all of the times he'd listened to her when she was grieving or encouraged her when past betrayals rose up and told her she wasn't good enough, she remembered.

She remembered too well.

The orchard was where he'd often come when he wanted some quiet time. Where he'd been just the day before, when he was trying to force his brain into remembering. Somewhere out here, he was either taking an ax to a dead tree or he was wandering among the rows, praying and thinking.

Praying. That was something she should do. After talking with her father, she'd fallen asleep on the couch, staring at the lights on the Christmas tree. Her dreams had been the queasiest blend of kisses and chaos, light and darkness, of her past with Ian and their present danger.

When she'd jolted awake at sunrise, it was with thoughts clarified by rest and driven by her father's words. She either trusted Ian or she didn't. Halfway wouldn't work. If she believed he was capable of derailing his life to make big money with bad men, that required her to believe he'd run a three-year con on her.

When she analyzed their work relation-ship and their personal relationship, she simply didn't see that sort of deception. If he could lie that well, then he had never been the man she *knew* he was.

So she'd chosen to trust, handing him the computer and his own program, the means to hack nearly any system in the world.

The look on his face told Makenzie that he understood the value of that gift.

Then panic had rocked him. He'd grown pale and bolted. She'd given him ten minutes of a head start, a few moments to himself, then she'd hopped in the farm truck and headed out.

On the last aisle before the orchard gave way to the acres of firs that made up the commercial tree farm, a flash of red revealed Ian's whereabouts. He was walking toward her up the row dividing apple trees from firs, an ax slung over his shoulder, his dark blond hair fallen out of its typical messy style and dropping over his forehead.

Makenzie's hands slipped from the steering wheel. Her heart skittered a couple of extra beats. It was really no wonder she'd once lost her head over him, had been willing to swerve her career sideways to see if two partners could become one heart. He was all sorts of muscular male wrapped up in flannel and blue jeans.

Any girl could be forgiven for noticing that.

You're not in high school. You're a grown woman. A federal agent. Stop acting the fool.

After reaching for the handle, she rolled down the window, which protested the movement at every turn. "You okay?"

He closed the last few feet between them and stowed the ax in the truck bed. Walking over to her, he then stood beside the door with his hands shoved into his pockets. "I don't know for sure. Maybe?"

Well, there really wasn't a more honest answer than that. He was so close that Makenzie could feel the warmth he radiated. So close she could reach out the window, pull him closer and lay her forehead against his, sharing his pain.

Or maybe transferring her memories to him. If it was possible, she would.

Instead, she rested her hands on the bottom of the steering wheel and pressed her fingers flat against the cracked vinyl. "What happened?"

The haunted look he'd worn so often since his rescue returned to his blue eyes, deepening them from summer sky to angry ocean. "I froze." He gripped the door with tight fingers and leaned back, stretching his arms. His gaze skittered away from hers toward the stand of Christmas trees.

That particular acreage looked like it might be ready for next Christmas.

What would twelve months from now look like for her, for Ian, given how the past twelve had gone off the rails in a thousand different ways? Given that she might choose to trust him, but the government would want evidence of innocence?

Bending his elbows, Ian eased closer to the truck, then crossed his forearms on the door. It should have looked relaxed, but his body was too tense. He searched her face, then looked down at his arms. His lips parted as though he was going to speak, but he stopped.

She really needed to stop noticing things like that.

This time, she couldn't help but touch him. Resting her hand on his forearm, she squeezed lightly. There had to be a way to take some of the pain from him. "I can't imagine what it's like to be in your head right now."

"No. You can't." His gaze rested on her hand on his arm. "It's like when you have a word on the tip of your tongue but you can't remember it. No matter how hard you try, you can't get it to come forward and be known. Only it's not a word. It's my life. It's...you."

Makenzie dug her teeth into her lower lip, biting back a gasp at the jolt to her heart. The way he said the words, he knew. The memories might not be there, but he knew her. Somehow.

"I want to remember you. You're right there. I can feel you, but I can't remember you."

Her fingers tightened against the soft flannel over his chilled arm. Her inhale was shy at best. It gave away everything she felt for him at worst.

"Noah gave me some good advice though."

"Noah?" At six, he could be a little precocious, but no way was he was doling out the deep life wisdom that an amnesiac federal agent might need.

"Right?" Ian's smile was slight but genuine. "Basically, if I stop trying to think so hard and just go for it, things will fall into place."

"Ah. The Noah Fuller soccer goalie strategy."

Ian chuckled, but the sound died. He eyed her for a moment as though he was making a decision, then dropped his gaze to the ground. "Earlier, I lied." His voice was a low rumble.

Adrenaline hit Makenzie's system. Hard. That voice, that demeanor... It was so "old Ian," when he knew who she was and who they were together. She dug her fingers into his arm so tightly, it was bound to cause him some pain, but she was terrified of letting him slip away again.

"I remembered something." When his head lifted suddenly, she wasn't ready. His eyes caught hers and held, almost the same way they had at the house the morning before.

Only this time, the pain had dissipated. In its place, a banked fire flared to life.

The same fire had sparked by the pond. A year ago.

He didn't close the distance between them this time. "What you said to Zane was true, wasn't it? I kissed you."

"You remember?" Her chest tightened, squeezing the question into a whisper.

"I don't know details, but I know how it… felt." Had his voice always been that low? That deep? "It didn't feel like you were my partner."

Her eyes closed and her mouth clamped shut. Maybe she should tell him the whole truth. Maybe—

"Mak?"

She opened her eyes as his fingers slipped past her neck and buried in her hair. His thumb brushed her cheek.

He was watching. Waiting.

For her.

THIRTEEN

Ian rested his forehead against hers and hesitated, his breath warm against her skin.

Feelings swamped him. Seeing her at gunpoint, praying as he'd rushed to her side that Nicholson hadn't pulled the trigger had shaken his already wobbly emotional equilibrium.

He was just foolish enough to kiss her.

A distant hum buzzed in his head. She was so close. If he kissed her, would it restore everything he'd lost?

He let his lips brush hers softly, and her grip on his arm tightened.

The black hole loomed.

Sudden fear rattled down his spine. He pulled away, staggered backward and stared at her, wide-eyed. The buzz died away.

Makenzie's expression matched his.

This feeling that he knew her while his brain said she was a stranger... It made the world tilt. The division between heart and mind made him feel as though, if he relaxed for even one second, he'd lose his identity into the darkness of the universe.

This made him feel even more untethered.

He heaved in oxygen, the cold air burning his lungs. How had he gotten here? They'd been talking about how he froze at the keyboard then—

"It's okay." Makenzie shoved the door open, the metal squealing a protest. Her voice was low, the kind someone would use to calm a frightened child. "Ian..." She eased closer and wrapped her arms around him, pressing her forehead to his shoulder. "It's okay."

Although his head warned him to pull away, his arms slipped around her, pressing her close. She was an anchor. The only thing that kept him from floating into nothingness.

What if Noah's strategy didn't work? The kid was only six, after all.

His earlier hope evaporated, floating away with the fir scent on the morning breeze.

What if the drug kept swelling until it engulfed all of the memories he still possessed? Until it destroyed him completely and left him a stranger to himself?

The longer they held each other with the slight whisper of the breeze through the fir trees the only sound between them, the more his thoughts quieted. The raging panic ebbed, though it left him feeling like a wrung-out washrag. "This is going to end eventually, right?"

"Eventually." Makenzie pulled away, letting cold air swirl between them. "I should never have let that happen. You're not in the headspace for anything personal about the two of us."

In the ebb tide of panic, his thoughts were almost too quiet and logical. He wanted to ask her for the truth about their past, but his brain had disengaged from his emotions. Logic said he couldn't handle the answer.

He needed to move. To walk. To, as Noah said, *stop thinking*.

But he didn't want to walk away from Makenzie, not when his emotional memory screamed that she was someone he should keep close.

He shoved his hands into his pockets. To the left, acres of fir trees darkened the day, offering shelter from the breeze and the opportunity to talk without having to look at each other. Now more than ever, she made him nervous, unsure what to do with his hands, how to arrange his face.

Kind of like when he was in middle school and asked Chloe Winston to the homecoming dance.

He cringed. Not the greatest analogy. Chloe had turned him down. Flat. In front of the entire cafeteria. Cured him of ever publicly asking a girl out again.

Why could he remember that and not Makenzie?

"What do you need?" Makenzie eyed him

with that way she had. It would do him well to remember she could read him better than he could read her. After all, she knew him.

There went that tremor along his spine again. *God, this can end at any time. Just zap back my life, please.*

Nothing. Maybe God wasn't in a *zapping* mood. Or maybe Ian was supposed to learn something from this whole mess.

That required more thought than he was ready for.

"Can we walk?" He pointed at the trees. "When I'm moving, things are clearer." What he needed more than his memories of Makenzie was the recollection of how to hack that computer. Answers might not restore his memory, but they might save his life.

And hers.

To do that, he needed to relax and stop trying to force his brain into submission.

That was so much harder than he'd thought it would be.

She nodded and fell into step beside him as they headed away from the apple trees into the taller fir trees. They walked deeper into manicured rows that smelled like Christmas.

His ears buzzed again, the sound hard to grasp. Was it inside his head or outside?

Makenzie shoved her hands into the pockets of her coat and walked toward the trees, seemingly oblivious.

Must be in his brain.

He let her get a few feet ahead. She wore jeans that hugged her legs and a black work coat. A cream-colored knit hat covered her dark hair, curls sticking out wildly beneath. If they'd dropped into one of those sappy holiday movies on TV, she'd fit right in.

He jogged to catch up, glancing down at his own attire as they wandered the lane of future Christmas trees that were about two feet taller than him. His plaid flannel shirt and jeans would probably qualify him for a starring movie role as well.

If only life had perfect endings.

The chill was less pronounced among the trees, where the breeze was blocked. If it wasn't cloudy, the air might not feel so icy, like a white Christmas was within reach.

"There's a reason it's been hard for me to trust you." Makenzie spoke so suddenly that Ian almost stopped walking.

For a moment, he'd forgotten everything except Christmas and her.

"I can tell you, if you want to hear it." She turned her face toward the sky. "Maybe if we talk about something other than your situation, it'll help your brain stop spinning."

"Is this a story I should know?"

"You've heard it before."

"Maybe it will snag a memory." He'd try anything. "Was it someone you were dating?" The thought didn't sit well. It brought a color to his emotions that matched the trees they strolled between.

"No." Her elbow brushed his arm, then she sidestepped to put more space between them. Tucking a strand of hair into her knit hat, she shrugged. "My soccer coach in college."

Ian balled his fists, anger surging hot

under his skin. The distant buzz sounded again, matching the hum in his emotions. The drive to protect her rocked through him so hard, he stumbled on the smooth dirt.

She didn't notice. Instead, her gaze was straight ahead as though she watched a movie from the past. "I was on a full-ride soccer scholarship to Sierra River University in Arizona. My dream college. I loved Coach Davies. She was like a mom to me, and that meant everything, having lost mine."

This was the story Zane had hinted at. Whatever had happened, it had piled on to the pain of her mother's death and furrowed deep scars.

"One day…" She sniffed and shoved her hands deeper into her pockets. "We were in the locker room after practice and in walked a bunch of people in suits. It was probably four or five but in my memory, it's like fifty. They cuffed her. Hauled her away in front of us."

Ian stopped walking. "Why?" He'd played baseball in college. He'd idolized and looked up to his coach. If Trevor Pierce had been unethical, it would have rocked Ian's faith in humanity. Maybe even in God.

"Illegal recruitment practices. Under-the-table deals with agents. Embezzlement from the athletic department. It was a huge scandal. Made national news." She trailed her fingers along the delicate needles of a fir tree, rubbing them between the pads of her fingers. "The NCAA shut down our program. The school revoked our scholar-ships. It was my senior year, so I didn't lose as much as some of the other players. A few had to drop out. Some were banned from playing elsewhere because they were aware of the illegal activities. Turned out I was involved, too, although I could prove I had no knowledge."

"How?"

"I was an all-conference and all-state player. I could have gone pro, had even had some conversations." She continued to press the needles together, intensifying the scent of Christmas around them. "There were some kickbacks to my high school coach for convincing me to choose Sierra River, and some money passed hands between Coach Davies and agents concerning me."

His heart squeezed. People she should have been able to trust had used her, betrayed her... Even her high school coaches had sold her future for their gain. He could only imagine the emotional fallout.

His disappearance must have ripped open old scars. Yet she'd moved forward. Continued with the Butler op. Charged ahead.

Alone.

She glanced at him, lifting a smile that held no joy. "Do you know what it's like to know you were a commodity? Every day, I've wondered about my coaches, Davies in particular. Did she really care about me? All those times I spilled my heart to her... Did she care? Or did she just want to win my trust so I'd listen when she made suggestions about my future? When she tried to steer me away from criminal justice into professional soccer?" She wrinkled her nose as though trying to hold back tears. "I almost scrapped my dream for hers. Every day I wonder about her motives."

An unspoken suspicion threaded through her words. She wondered about his motives, too. "Mak, I—"

"It took forever for me to trust Audra. I kept waiting for her to use me for gain, but all she ever did was mentor me and listen to me." She sniffed and rolled her eyes toward the snow-heavy clouds. "It's because of her that I ever trusted you in the first place."

What a gut punch. While he had no idea where he'd gone, he could only imagine the damage his apparent betrayal had done to her.

He hated the self he couldn't remember.

Without caring that he shouldn't, Ian grasped her forearm and pulled her close. He wanted to take away the stiffness in her stance and the pain in her eyes, especially after she'd reached out to him earlier, taking nothing, only giving.

She stepped into his embrace, and he felt for the first time since the hospital like he could offer something of value.

Like he had worth. It was all wrapped up in the warmth of Makenzie Fuller against his chest.

The buzzing in his ears rose again.

Stiffening, Makenzie pulled away and lifted her head, turning toward the sound.

The sadness in her expression shifted to concern. She stepped into the center of the aisle and scanned the clouds. "Do you hear that?"

"Been hearing it off and on for a while. Thought it was my brain."

As the humming grew louder, Makenzie reached beneath her jacket and withdrew a pistol he hadn't realized she was carrying. "If that's your brain, then whatever you have going on is contagious."

The noise rose in intensity, and a dark shadow approached over the firs.

A drone.

An *armed* drone.

Grabbing his arm, Makenzie dove between the trees, dragging him to the next row as bullets slammed into the ground where he'd been standing.

No cover. No cover. No cover.

Makenzie scanned the skies as the drone neared, honing in on its targets.

The fir trees were only a couple of feet taller than them. The trunks were thin and, while the branches would hide them, they would offer little protection.

They had to get out of sight.

The hum grew louder as the drone dropped lower, likely seeking better aim now that it had their location.

Makenzie dragged Ian behind a fir tree as another bullet buried itself in the thick branches beside them. Wood splintered. Needles exploded like confetti.

After letting go of Ian's arm, she shoved him forward, sprinting down the row and cutting across the next one toward the apple orchard a hundred yards away. The apple trees provided even less cover, but they needed to get closer to the truck before whoever was operating that drone sent it skyward again for a wider view.

If the drone picked up the truck near the boundary between the orchard and the tree farm, it would likely hover there, blocking their best chance of escape. It was a long way to the house, and she still had no cell.

They were on their own.

Behind them, the pitch of the drone changed, whining higher as the device shot upward, searching for their hiding place.

They pressed into the limbs of a broad fir, the needles pricking their skin and the sap sticking to their clothes. It was like drowning in Christmas.

Aside from the hum of the drone, the only sound was their breathing as they fought adrenaline and exertion.

Makenzie took a knee, aiming her side-arm in the direction of the drone's low hum. She glanced at Ian. "You okay? Not hit?" He'd been so weak as the drugs had worn off. Although he seemed much stronger today, it might be that too much exertion could derail him.

He appeared to be his old self though. At least physically. "I'm good. You?"

Eyeing the sky, Makenzie nodded once. Other than her blood pressure shooting for the stars, she was fine.

The drone was out of sight, and she didn't dare peek for fear of being spotted. If she could see the drone, then whoever was on the other side of its camera could easily see her. She could take a shot based on her hearing, but hitting a moving target while firing blind wouldn't be easy.

It was a bad idea anyway. A shot would give away their position.

"I know I'm missing four years of my life, but it's still illegal to arm a drone, right?" Ian was breathing heavily. He might be holding up, but it was clear he was still taxed from his ordeal.

It wasn't like Makenzie was feeling so great herself. "Yep. Still illegal, but since when are criminals concerned with legalities?" While she hadn't seen one, she'd heard rumblings about Butler's organization owning several commercial-grade drones, some equipped with light weaponry.

Slide those rumors over to the *verified* column.

"In the four years you don't remember, drones have upped their game. Some companies are using them to make deliveries in cities, so they can handle a heavier payload that bad actors can use to add on crude armaments."

"It doesn't have to be sophisticated to kill you," Ian muttered.

Truer words were never spoken. She hoped the thing wasn't outfitted with infrared, or their heat signatures would give them away even if they stayed out of sight.

"I'm guessing you aren't holstering an extra pistol anywhere." Ian's voice over her shoulder was almost bitter.

She could only guess how helpless he was feeling. Again. If she was in his shoes, unarmed, protected instead of protecting... Well, she might charge out and start throwing rocks at that aerial menace, David-and-Goliath style.

Come to think of it… She looked over her shoulder at him. "Don't even think about it."

Even given their situation, he had the good nature to look a little sheepish. "No rocks, huh?"

"No rocks."

The hum of the drone's engine dimmed as it drifted away from them, searching.

It would be back.

Tightening her grip on her Sig, she glanced at Ian. "How long were you hearing it before it spotted us?"

"Maybe five? A little more?" He backed closer into the limbs of the tree as the vehicle's pitch indicated it was gaining altitude, searching a wider area. "I got a quick look at it. It's not a big drone. Unless batteries have come a long way in the past four years, it will have limited flight time. How limited, I can't say. There weren't a lot of things coming up the pipeline as far as batteries, at least that I remember. A lot depends on the weight of the additional armaments and their drain on the system. Then again, I could be way off and this thing could fly for days."

Well, he certainly hadn't forgotten his tech skills. That was good, because other than saying, *it flies up and comes down again*, she couldn't tell anyone how a drone worked. "So do we make a run for it or wait this thing out?"

"I say we run. If it's got even ten minutes of juice left, that's enough to eventually find us and take us out. Be glad that thing's not toting a machine gun."

Then they'd really be toast. "So we make a run for the truck." It seemed their best chance at surviving. "With the height he's got, he'll see us the instant we move."

"Then we have to run fast. Or..." Ian half stood, pressing close to the tree. "I've got a better idea?"

It was a question. Would she treat him like a trusted partner or a suspected traitor?

In their situation, she'd forgotten he wasn't her partner. They'd fallen into the easy camaraderie and group-think they'd once shared. It was too dangerous for her to shove him away now. "What are you thinking?"

The drone hummed louder as it dipped in altitude and flew closer. They only had a few seconds.

Ian eased to standing, letting his head move out of the cover of the tree's branches. "I'm not thinking. I'm just doing."

Now was not the time to take a six-year-old's life advice. "Get down!"

The hum raised in intensity when the drone picked up speed.

Ian had been spotted.

He looked down at her. "I'll draw fire. You take him out."

Before she could argue with the stupidity of the idea, Ian stepped into the center of the aisle between the rows, looked directly at the drone, then turned and ran away from the truck.

He'd lost what was left of his mind.

The air rang with the sound of gunfire as the drone operator tried to get a clear shot.

Lord, keep him safe.

Sliding sideways, still on one knee, Makenzie steadied herself and got a bead on the drone.

The craft was too far away and moving too fast. Too erratically. Ian needed to bring it this way so she could get a bead on it.

As if he'd heard her thoughts, the sound of Ian's footsteps stopped then drew closer as he doubled back toward her. She couldn't see him, but she sure could hear him.

The drone fired again, sweeping lower as it honed in on its prey.

Right…into…position…

Makenzie sighted and fired. The recoil of the Sig shocked through her hand.

She fired again.

The drone hovered, hesitating.

It turned toward her, swooping lower.

It had her in its sights.

Well, she wasn't moving.

"Makenzie! Take cover!" Ian crashed between the trees toward her.

She wasn't backing down. This ended now.

Leveling her weapon as the drone hummed nearer, she took aim…
And fired.

FOURTEEN

What was Makenzie thinking? Ian pushed faster, trying to reach her.

So he could what? Throw himself between her and a bullet?

Yeah. Exactly that.

Her shot cracked the air at the same moment the drone fired again… This time at her.

The ground to Makenzie's left exploded in dirt and fir needles.

The air grew eerily quiet.

A moment of silence ended in an extended crash as the drone hit multiple tree limbs before it thudded to the ground.

Ian stopped running, his foot sliding on needles that dropped him almost into a split before he landed on one knee. His mouth hung open. Had she just… Just shot a drone? Out of the sky?

Whoa. Remind him not to get on her bad side.

Makenzie scrambled to her feet, pistol still aimed at the drone, and crept forward. "Ian, take cover. It's on the ground but it might not be—"

A force zipped past his arm and a gunshot cracked. He dropped and rolled behind a tree, grabbing for his arm as he came up.

The sleeve of his shirt was ripped, but no blood or pain said he'd been hit.

That was entirely too close.

"You hit?" Makenzie kept her eye on the drone as she circled around to the left.

"No." He could explain the scorched hole in her dad's shirt later, when they were somewhere safe.

If they ever found where that was.

Makenzie moved from tree to tree about twenty feet away from him, flanking the mechanical assassin.

Pulling in deep breaths to steady himself, Ian peeked around the tree at the drone, which had landed about fifteen feet from him. It was face up, battered but not destroyed. One of the blade mounts was shattered where Makenzie's bullet had found its mark.

The small gun mount still turned.

It was tracking Makenzie.

"Mak. Stop moving."

Immediately, she froze behind the tree she'd been about to step around. "What's up?"

"It's not firing blind. It can see you."

Tilting her head back in an exasperated move Ian almost recognized, she slowly aimed her weapon at the ground. "It has to run out of bullets eventually."

"Yeah? How many does it have left? Have you been counting? Because I haven't." Ian dragged his hand down his face. He'd drawn fire once. He could do it again. "It's likely built with a 360-degree field of view, but given the way it came to rest, I might be in a blind spot."

"*Might* be? You wanna take that chance?" She eyed him across the row. "Normally

I'd lay down suppressive fire, but you can't scare a robot into ducking for cover." She rolled her eyes heavenward. "I'm literally fighting a robot. Didn't have that on my career bingo card."

"Focus, Fuller." Was she always like this? Humor in the midst of danger? It wasn't the first time she'd cracked a joke.

"Okay. Look." She shifted as though she was making a stand. "You're the tech whiz, right? I'll draw fire. You take out the Terminator."

No way. Makenzie was not going to be the one in the crosshairs. He couldn't let her sacrifice her life for his. He had a feeling his forgotten self would eventually remember and would never forgive him.

He was pretty sure his present self would feel the pain, too.

Focus, Andrews. This was not the time for that rabbit trail. He shifted position, trying to come up with a way to stop her.

"I see you forming an argument. No time for that. You have five seconds to look at that thing and see if you can figure out how to disarm it, then I'm moving."

"Mak, I— What if I can't figure it out?" He could freeze again.

If he did, Makenzie could die.

"Don't think. Just do."

This was different than running in front of a drone. This required him to remember buried skills. "Mak—"

"Five…"

She was serious.

She was also right. He was the tech guy. This was something he'd known *before* his memory blip. He could do this.

As her *four* rang among the trees, he scanned the machine.

By the time she hit *one*, he knew what needed to be done.

He hoped.

Makenzie darted from one tree to the next, and Ian sprinted for the drone.

The small gun turret spun then stopped to fire.

Needles flew from the tree Makenzie had ducked behind, but she appeared to be safe.

Sliding on his knees, Ian reached for the drone as the turret spun toward him.

He'd been spotted.

With a whispered prayer and sheer adrenaline, he reached for the main wire he'd identified. It had better be the right one or he would take a bullet at point-blank range.

He winced against the blow and pulled.

The turret stopped. The gun remained silent.

The monster was dead.

Opening his eyes slowly, Ian stared at the barrel of the gun pointed directly at him. With an exhale that ruffled the fir needles on the tree closest to him, Ian dropped to his backside away from the gun and let his chin fall to his chest. Closing his eyes, he rested his wrists on his bent knees.

That was too close.

Makenzie walked across the aisle and stood over him. "You okay?"

They were asking that question way too often. "Just convincing my heart it can still beat in rhythm." He opened his eyes to look up at her, but he caught a glimpse of her shoes before he could lift his head.

A flash of memory. A different pair of boots. Cobblestones. Danger.

Scrambling backward, he jumped to his feet. Sudden wooziness made the ground wobble.

Makenzie reached for him. "What's wrong?" Stepping in front of him, she gripped his shoulders, scanning his head, his chest, his arms. "Were you hit?"

"No. Just... I remembered something." He lifted his chin and met her gaze. Why was he constantly having weak moments in front of her? He should be stronger than this. Should be able to wrestle his memory from the ether it had vanished into.

He shouldn't be panicking at every turn.

She was studying his face, more concerned than suspicious.

That was a first.

"What did you remember?" She was close. With her hands on his shoulders that way, it was awfully similar to an embrace.

Too close.

He shook his head and gently backed away from her. "Boots. Cobblestones. The feeling I was in trouble."

She dropped her hands and turned away to crouch in front of the drone, inspecting it. "There were cobblestones when Butler was dragging you to his car. When I walked up, you couldn't look up from the ground. I was wearing boots. As for danger?" She poked at the drone and tested its weight. The thing was about two feet square and likely heavy. "We're still in that."

Yes, they were, but not at this second.

Unless another drone was winging toward them. "That thing's toast. I ripped out the main circuit wires."

"Yeah, but someone knows where we are. They've proved the fences my dad built can't keep them out." She stood and wiped her hands together, staring down at the drone. "Just wait until I tell him he's going to need antiaircraft weapons now." She chuckled bitterly as furrows dug into her forehead. "I'm glad Zane is getting Noah out of here."

The sooner the better. It was likely that whoever had put targets on their chests would come after her family in order to hurt her.

He didn't even want to think about Makenzie's nephew in danger.

Shifting to a crouch, Ian scanned the drone. It wasn't military-grade machinery. "You were right about what you said earlier. Someone modified a commercial drone to carry a weapon."

"How does that happen?"

"You can find a lot of things on the Dark Web." He should know. He'd spent more than his fair share of time hunting down killers, traffickers and terrorists in the shadowy corners of the internet where evil thrived.

Makenzie frowned. "With all of the arms at Butler's disposal, why would he hack civilian equipment?"

"Well, again, I'm operating on a four-year lag, but last I knew, military drones weren't very portable for the average arms dealer. They're huge. They require specialized training, transport and fuel. This one is easy to move and fly, unlike a military bird. It was probably going to run out of battery before it ran out of bullets."

"What's the range on that thing?"

He shrugged and hefted the drone, leaning it to the side as he eyed its components. "Two miles? Maybe?"

"So they know exactly where we are *and* they're close." Makenzie pointed to a handle along the device's support structure. "Grab a side. We'll carry it to the truck, take it to the house, then we have to make a plan."

"Wait."

She stopped in midreach and looked up at him from beneath her lashes.

"Leave it here for now. If there's any kind of tracker in it and we move it, then it could lead someone straight to us."

"They've already found us."

"Better to leave them with a general area than to paint a target directly on ourselves."

Chewing her lower lip, Makenzie stared at the drone, then seemed to make a decision. "Okay. Let's get out of the open though."

They hurried to the truck, ears tuned to the sky.

Makenzie drove quickly but carefully over the uneven ground, passing through the center of the apple orchard and avoiding the main avenue that ran closer to the road at the edge of the property. She seemed to be watching all directions, and her teeth continued to work her lower lip.

She was planning. It was another thing he knew without knowing how he knew.

"What are you thinking?" When he broke the silence, his voice seemed loud.

"A lot of things." The truck coasted on a straight stretch of gravel-packed drive when she lifted her foot from the gas. Looking over at him, she shook her head. "We're losing. And while my dad likes his security toys and was trained as a SEAL, it's been a while since he's had to fight. He was an analyst and a cryptographer. I'm not sure I want him in a gun battle."

"You're considering running?"

"Maybe."

"Let's think it through. You said it yourself. Your dad's built a fortress. If we can stay out of sight of any more drones, then we have an edge. We've got the space and time to get into those laptops." He had to try again. They were out of options.

She had to know that a killer might come after her family just to make a statement, whether they sheltered in place or not.

"I guess." He was breaking her down. Her posture eased, though the lines in her forehead and around her mouth etched deeper.

"We can make a stand here, Mak. Maybe even manage to take some of them into custody if they breach the perimeter." He balled his fists and pressed them into his thighs. There was nowhere else they could be safe. Where *she* could be safe. "Let's stop running and end this. Today."

Ian stood at the office window and stared over the orchard, peering through a crack in the heavy curtains at skies growing heavy with clouds. From the house's vantage point at the top of the hill, the land rolled away and the view stretched for miles.

No shadow soared toward the house or toward Zane's SUV, which disappeared into the trees as it wended up the driveway toward the main road.

He'd rest a whole lot easier once Noah was out of harm's reach. Makenzie would, too.

Behind him at her father's desk, Makenzie quietly retrieved the laptops from the safe where she'd stashed them when she'd chased after him. Before he'd brushed a barely there kiss across her lips. One he could still feel.

Before they'd almost been killed.

Although the scene in front of him was peaceful now, someone had launched a drone with lethal capability from within his sight. It was a crude mockup, small but effective.

It didn't take *big* to do damage. After all, in the Bible, the future king David had taken down a giant with some stones and a sling. Then again, David had God's backing.

He hoped he was the David and not the Goliath.

With one last scan of the sky, he dropped the curtain and faced the office, letting his gaze sweep past Makenzie where she drew the chair closer to the desk.

He focused instead on the laptops she'd opened. He tilted his head from side to side, but it did nothing to ease the tension in his neck and shoulders. Nothing would ease that until this was over.

It seemed *over* hinged on him putting his hands on that keyboard and doing what he did best.

Maybe if he could get his brain to act like a kindergartner defending a soccer goal… *I just do better when I don't think. When I just play.*

Okay, then. He was going to crack the password on that computer.

At the desk, he sat down with a new resolve to not be, well, resolved.

"You going in?" Makenzie was typing on her laptop as though everything didn't rest on what Ian was about to do.

"Yep." He appreciated her acting as though this was any other moment on any other mission they'd worked together, although he was pretty sure this didn't look or feel like any of the others.

Powering up the machine, Ian rested his hands on the keyboard and closed his eyes. If he'd done this as many times as he guessed he had, then there would be some sort of muscle memory lying dormant inside him. Similar to the kind that had made Gage have to pretend to dial when someone asked him for a phone number. Action drove his partner's memory.

His *former* partner's memory.

Ian pulled in several deep breaths through his nose, then opened his eyes and clicked on the dialog box.

Waited.

Nothing. The black hole of his memory loomed large.

He closed his eyes and tried to ignore the void. The goal was to relax and let his mind drift.

At a soft sound behind him, he nearly

opened his eyes, but he focused on Makenzie typing beside him. On the way her presence carried the slight scent he had come to recognize as simply being her. On the way she breathed as she gave him space.

These were things he'd been so busy struggling to remember that he'd blocked them from his mind. Now, in self-imposed darkness, freeing his senses to play, memories rushed in.

Of sitting in the front seat of his car on a stakeout. Of some sort of Christmas party here at the farm. Of the moment he'd spotted her at the wedding two nights ago.

That memory brought a quick flash of fear. Not for him, but for her.

Had he known she was in danger? What was he doing there in the first place?

He squeezed his eyes tighter, then relaxed against the circling panic. *Stop forcing it.* He focused on the low hum of the laptop fans. His thumb tapped the smooth trackpad. His fingers drifted to the keyboard, lingering over the raised edge on the *J* key.

A line of code slipped through his mind.

His eyes flew open as memory rushed in. He might not remember the last four years, but he knew how to use this program. Clicking through menus, he opened another dialog box, typed. Waited on the program to do its job. Then...

With one last punch to the enter key, he turned in his seat and faced Makenzie head-on and triumphant. His knee brushed hers where she sat watching. "I'm in."

Makenzie grabbed his wrist and leaned closer. "I knew you could do it." The pride in her expression just about dropped him from his chair.

Their noses were only inches apart. Their eyes locked. His entire world narrowed into the space between them.

Nothing else existed. No black hole. No looming assassin. Just her. Just him, desperate for her to believe in him, even though he couldn't remember the last time she had.

He swallowed emotions he couldn't put names to. "Did you?" The words cracked and eked out as a whisper.

He'd been here before. This close to her. Not just on the deck the day before or in the orchard earlier. At some other point in the past, in a moment he couldn't visualize, he'd breathed the same air as her. Had shared the same thoughts.

Something simmered between them, just beneath the surface. More than their professional partnership and more than a single kiss. If he stopped thinking about it, started feeling it, he could almost see the past on the edges of his mind's eye.

Not that their past was all they had. This moment was incredible in its own right.

Makenzie wasn't backing away from him the way she should.

The way *he* should.

She nodded, but her eyes never left his. "I've always believed you could do anything you wanted to do."

The urge to drown in her was even stronger than it had been earlier. Every time she was close, the pull grew more intense.

The same questions hovered between them. Without answers, those questions and suspicions would remain a buffer that drove them apart.

More than anything, he wanted to answer the questions about his past so that he could put them to rest and finally close the gap between him and Makenzie.

It took a herculean effort, but he turned away from her and rested his hands on the keyboard. "Let's find out what Storm is so desperate to bury that he'll kill to keep it hidden."

FIFTEEN

He'd hacked into a laptop with the same skill he'd always possessed and she'd always admired.

For one moment, after the laptop accepted the password, he'd looked at her with an expression that charged through her. He knew her. Knew her better than anyone.

That man she'd loved was in there. He existed. Their promises to one another were still banked somewhere in his memory.

Promises he'd broken. Her jaw tightened as her body tensed.

She kept forgetting that part. In all of the teamwork and the rhythm of working together, her heart kept forgetting that he'd been able to turn his back on everything they'd personally been to one another without saying a word.

Maybe amnesia was contagious.

As Ian turned to the computer, she rolled her chair away from the desk and walked to the window to peek between the curtains.

The sunshine from previous days had fittingly vanished. The sky hung ever heavier with clouds that promised Christmas snow.

Makenzie dropped the curtain into place and studied the whorled pattern in the fabric. This constant war between her head and her heart, between her professional investigation and her personal life had left her queasy, like a roller coaster going so fast it was about to jump the tracks.

God, why can't I just land in one place? Trust him...or not? I keep thinking it's resolved, then it isn't.

Forget being on the job for thirty seconds. She wanted to have the conversation they kept dancing around. The near misses and the heartrending *almosts* had to stop.

After that brief glimpse of him, she wanted to know for certain that the man she'd fallen in love with still knew who she was. That she was important enough to live inside him even though he'd forgotten everything else.

If she knew that, then she could focus on work.

The only sound in the room was their breathing. Ian had stopped working, probably remembering better than she had that he couldn't touch the machine without her supervision if they wanted to maintain an aboveboard investigation.

Because that was the kind of guy he was.

She walked over and looked down at him across the desk. "These moments where we get close… There's something inside you about us. Do you remember any of it?"

He sank into the chair and stared at the laptop. "I don't know. When you and I are close, that's when I start to feel like I can remember who I am." He stood and leaned his fists on the desktop, bringing them eye to eye, the desk the only thing between them. "What's the whole truth about us?"

The room darkened with the rapidly approaching weather. When she was a kid, that first hint of snow always spun her into a desperation familiar to many kids in the South. Would it turn into one of those rare storms bringing snow that would last for days?

Or would it flurry just long enough to dust the ground before vanishing in a disappointing mush of damp grass and wet dirt?

Like this moment.

As much as they both needed to hear the truth, she couldn't bear it if the flurry left her with nothing but mud. She might have trusted him with that laptop, but she wasn't ready to trust him with her heart, not when it kept beating that he'd left her once and he could do it again.

She'd been disposable too often to people she'd cared about. Even Audra had betrayed her by dying.

"Forget it." Instead of running toward the finish line she desperately wanted to reach, she veered down a side road. "None of that is important until we know who wants us dead." Reaching across the desk, she turned the laptop he'd unlocked toward her. "We need to find out what Storm had to say."

Although she focused on the screen, she could see Ian from the corner of her eye. He looked stunned, almost as though she'd thrown a bucket of cold snow at him. With a quick inhale, he seemed to center himself. "Check emails first. See if there's a messaging program."

Investigative technique 101. The quickest way to find answers was to look for communications. They both knew it. Likely, he was saying it just to put his brain into place as much as she'd had to square her shoulders to remember why she was here.

"There's no messaging app installed and no emails in the program." They could be buried somewhere. Her computer skills, while impressive, were rudimentary next to Ian's.

While her heart was wary, her head knew that four years earlier, Ian was a competent investigator.

Makenzie turned the computer toward him and walked around to stand behind him. "Work your magic."

It only took a few keystrokes before several windows popped up. Ian pulled his hands from the keyboard and stared. "The actual operating system is buried behind a dummy."

Makenzie sat on the edge of the chair and tried not to notice how animated he was when he was in his element.

Ian slid the computer over to her. "There's basically a whole other laptop behind what you can see from a cursory glance. Whoever built this was good. Maybe even better than me."

She glanced sideways at his lighthearted arrogance. It was so *Ian.*

But the only way to do this was to remain professional, pretending that nothing personal hovered between them.

A series of texts populated a messaging app at the side of the screen. There were dozens from an unknown user. Instructions for digital currency transactions. Dates for future meets with buyers, including one for the next week in Nashville. If Storm didn't realize they'd hacked the system, this was gold. They knew exactly where to be and when.

In one message, the anonymous sender referred to a "script" in an email.

Makenzie pulled up the email server Ian had uncovered and scanned it. Multiple emails with the subject line *Script for...* and names of buyers Makenzie had been tracking. Buyers that Butler had sold to. Had wined and dined.

She opened one of the scripts and read through it, dread pooling heavy and cold in her stomach. She'd sat in on some of these meetings and listened to Butler operate.

He'd been smooth and convincing, wooing buyers.

The entire time, he'd been following a script written by someone else.

How had she missed it? For nearly a year, she'd worked her way up through Robert Butler's organization until she was his right arm. Her entire team had been so certain he was the lead man of his organization that they'd set up this deep cover op to take him down.

They'd been wrong.

"What is it?" Ian leaned closer.

No doubt he'd seen the way her hands had frozen on the keyboard. She couldn't pull them away. "Butler was a puppet." She convinced her frozen fingers to scroll through more emails. "He was never in charge. All of the evidence pointed to him but he was a ventriloquist's dummy, only saying what these scripts told him to say. Someone else is pulling the strings." She dragged her hands down her face. She'd been conned, exactly like Butler's puppet master intended. Whoever Storm was, he'd been the ringleader all along.

She'd been duped again.

"Mak?" Ian was staring at the screen. "What's that unopened email from two days ago?"

The subject line screamed in all caps. *URGENT!*

Her heart twisting over itself, Makenzie clicked on the email.

Phrases jumped out of the message. *Never should have left you in charge while I was*

overseas... You trusted the wrong person...
Undercover agent... Sending a cleaner to
take care of the problem...

She clicked the small paper clip that indicated two photo attachments, already knowing she'd see her own face.

A copy of her credentials popped up on the screen. She'd been the target all along. The threat to Ian's life was to draw her away from the reception. Butler had multiple backup options whenever he killed. Somehow, Ian had been caught in the crosshairs.

Unfortunately for him, this one had backfired.

As the second image opened, her gut twisted over on itself.

The "cleaner" was Ian.

Ian shoved out of the chair and threw his hands into the air. He backed against the corner of the L-shaped desk, even as Makenzie rocketed from her seat. He knew what was coming, and it sickened him to the core.

She aimed her gun straight at him, stepping out of arms' reach.

"Whoa. Mak. No." His throat went dry. While he'd had a handful of weapons aimed in his direction, they'd never been drawn so quickly or been held by someone he had feelings for. "I know this looks really bad." Did it ever. Any trust she'd had in him evaporated in the nuclear bomb of those photos.

They had to be wrong. He'd never do that to her.

If he was in her shoes though, he'd probably have the same gut reaction.

"You were sent to kill me." Her voice was ice. Jagged, breaking ice. "That's why you were at the reception."

This was all wrong. No matter who he'd become, there was no way he'd fallen that far. "You know better. That's not who I am."

Except that in that video, he'd seen his expression when he spotted her. He could feel the fear. Could it have been because he was sent to kill her?

No. He still couldn't imagine a scenario where he'd flip from hacker to assassin. Their teams were built specifically with one techie and one weapons expert. In the past, Ian had been the brains and Gage had been the muscle. He assumed the same had been true of his partnership with Makenzie.

She was, after all, very quick on the draw.

Still, he didn't think Makenzie would shoot him. Her finger wasn't even on the trigger.

That didn't make a gun aimed at his center mass any less terrifying.

"It's right there on the screen, Ian." Holding her aim, Makenzie turned the laptop toward him with her free hand. The pain in her expression tore at his heart. She'd already lost so much, been betrayed so deeply...

Wait. If someone had figured out who Makenzie was and knew they were on the run together, then the logical next step would be to turn them against each other. They were already isolated from her team. Leaving her without him would play upon her fears of abandonment and betrayal in ways that were downright vindictive.

He kept his hands up as he eyed the screen, reread the email and scanned the photos. Something was off.

He tilted his head toward the screen. "May I?"

Makenzie chewed her bottom lip, her glare as hot as her words had been cold.

"Look, if I wanted to kill you, I've had a dozen chances already." He prayed with his whole heart she'd listen to reason and not let her emotions drive her response. "I can prove this is fake. Someone wants you to think I'm your bad guy."

Makenzie lowered the pistol, but she didn't holster it. "I hope you're right." Defeat weighted her words like never before. She stood rigidly, watching him.

Lowering his hands slowly, Ian rested his fingers on the table in front of the laptop. "First, these are the photos from our credentials. Hacking into the system could get anyone access to those. If this was real, they would have provided recent photos, proof that you were undercover. They wouldn't have sent my government photo. That would make the whole thing reek of a setup."

Makenzie stared at the screen, a dozen emotions playing across her face before she looked at him. "If Butler had this information before the wedding, I'd have been dead before the vows." Slowly, she holstered her weapon. "Plus it makes no sense for you to be killed if you're the hired killer." She shook her head and stepped closer, still maintaining distance. "Whoever initiated this whole thing gave the order from that car outside of the castle just before the ball started rolling. This email isn't it."

Ian scanned the screen, practiced eyes searching for clues. "I can prove it's fake." He slid the cursor to the header. "According to the date, the email was sent two days ago, on the morning of the wedding." He clicked some drop-down menus and navigated to the dialog box that opened the full email header.

There it was. He pointed at the dateline.

The email had actually been sent today, only six hours earlier. "Someone spoofed the incoming time stamp, but they couldn't fool the main server. Whoever they are, they're good."

Makenzie cleared her throat. "But not as good as you?"

"Not as good as me." The answer was reflexive, without thought.

She sniffed what might have been a laugh. "You remember that." Her voice was soft, accepting.

She'd let go of the idea he was hired to murder her.

"I remember what?"

"It was something you'd say all the time. You could be a little arrogant about your skill set. You could never acknowledge that anyone might be better than you." She waved a hand as though brushing away the memory.

If only he had the luxury of memories to brush away.

"Anyway, something of us is still in your head." Makenzie stared at the computer screen, where the condemning "evidence" looked back at her. "I'm sorry I aimed a weapon at you."

"I'm sorry you had to." He shifted in his seat, angling toward her. "So, what else should be in my brain about us?" He'd like to let it go. She'd made it clear she wasn't going to talk about it no matter how hard he pushed.

After reaching for the laptop, she started to close it. "You deactivated the login password?"

So she was just going to ignore him? He should have known. "Yes."

With a nod, she shut the computer, stacked it on top of her own and stood. "I'm going to take a breather then comb through these and see what other evidence I can find. If Storm is really the mastermind behind everything, we'll have to dig into who he could be."

"Could it be someone in the organization already?" It would make sense they'd want to stay close to Butler, possibly even make themselves seem to be subservient to him.

If that was the case, then who was in the car?

Makenzie hesitated at the door. "Could be. I mean, if it is, that would mean even a complete lunk like Cale Nicholson might be the big boss. It's possible his *I hate your guts for getting promoted ahead of me* anger was an act." She half smiled. "Then again, he managed to get caught, so I doubt he's our guy." She tapped her fingers on the laptop she held against her chest. "Storm mentioned being out of the country. If that's true, then maybe Butler was holding down the fort in his stead. Or maybe he has a dozen Butlers around the world, fronting for him. If one gets caught, the organization still stands."

"So you have to cut off the head of the dragon, not just its arm?"

"Exactly." With a nod, Makenzie disappeared, her footsteps fading up the hall.

Storm could be anyone, but whoever it was clearly had ties to their unit. Whether they were part of Overwatch or had a mole on the inside, he had no idea. It was clear someone close knew about their shared past, the safe house and Makenzie's family.

Come to think of it, those were all things he'd have known.

He shook off the idea that he could be the mole. That kind of change in his personality and values was too huge to consider.

Leaning back in the chair, Ian stared at the curtains. Too much was happening too fast. With his brain still distantly achy and desperately foggy, he was lagging behind. His innocence and name were on the line.

Whatever his relationship with Makenzie had been, it was clearly on the line as well.

Closing his eyes, he framed each of the memory flashes he'd had so far, trying to flesh them out, to live in the moments.

The one that persistently shoved its way to the front was that kiss he'd first seen. The one he'd first felt.

After shoving out of the chair, Ian paced the room, feeling as though he was locked up.

In a way he was locked in the past. Maybe even imprisoned in the future if he couldn't figure out where he'd been and what he'd been doing for the last year.

He stopped in front of the bookcase, reading titles, scanning photos of Makenzie and her family through the years. It seemed every photo of Noah featured his prized soccer ball.

No wonder he was a "projidy."

He skimmed the photos until he came to one of Makenzie and another woman at what seemed to be a promotion or awards ceremony. They were smiling at the camera and were clearly close. Like Makenzie, the other woman had short dark hair that waved just past her chin. She was older than Makenzie and carried an air of—

Memories slammed him with a force that nearly rocked him off his feet.

Grabbing for the bookcase, Ian gripped the wooden shelf, holding on for fear of his knees giving way.

It came back. All of it. In an earthquake that rocked the foundations of his world. He sank into a leather chair and stared at the photo.

He'd never met Major Audra Robinson.

He *had* met Storm.

And he was looking at her photo.

Gathering himself, he stood and placed the picture onto the shelf, staring at the woman whose lips smiled at the camera while her eyes did not. She'd been deeply entrenched in Overwatch before she'd been wooed away by the draw of more money. She'd faked her own death, pinned it on India Garrison and taken over the other woman's organization. India's own hacker had switched up the DNA and dental records that had identified "Audra's" body.

Then her hacker was killed in a freak accident.

Audra had hired Ian.

Disoriented by the sudden crash of memory, he walked to the office door and stared up the hall. He had no doubt that it had been Audra in that car outing them to Robert Butler. She'd definitely discovered that Makenzie was undercover in the Butler organization. When she'd figured out Makenzie was involved, she'd likely questioned Ian's motives and loyalty.

Makenzie was already on fragile ground concerning him. He couldn't go to her with the truth about Audra. Not now. It could destroy everything.

None of that mattered. One year of surveilling Makenzie. Two years of waiting. One year of working.

A nightmare scenario that had nearly cost him everything.

He had a job to do. He had credibility to earn if he was going to finish what he'd started.

Stepping lightly to the phone on the desk, he lifted the receiver and dialed the number he'd committed to memory.

A woman answered. "You have a lot to explain."

"I will." *Eventually.*

"Are you ready to take her down?"

His eyes slipped shut. This was going to be harder than he'd ever imagined. Swallowing, he nodded. "Yes."

SIXTEEN

A rapid *beep* floated dimly up the hallway, like an old alarm clock awaking from snooze.

Makenzie blinked and looked up, shoving the laptop away from where she sat cross-legged on her bed.

She'd been staring at both machines for too long, trying to make sense of coded messages and hidden emails. She'd bounced between her intel on the cloud and the hard intel on the laptop Storm had provided to Butler, but she couldn't match things up the way she needed to. She was intelligent, but she also needed Ian's expertise. While she was gifted with tactical thinking and problem-solving skills, he had a way of looking at data that went beyond what other people could see. He could read a line of code and know immediately if it was out of place or if it held the key to an encrypted system.

That wasn't in her scope of training.

The beeping continued, and she stretched her neck, glancing at her watch. It was close to dinner time. Her mind was mush, and she needed food then rest. She should check on Ian and find something to eat.

Except she didn't trust herself around Ian, not in the state she was in. Exhaustion made her weak. It made her brain run in circles she didn't want it to run in.

It made her heart bust down the walls and let her know with stark clarity that, despite her best efforts not to, she still loved Ian. Had never stopped. He was still the man she'd planned to detour her career for. When he looked at her the way he had multiple times, with that expression that said his heart still knew who she was...

It was enough to make her forget.

"Makenzie!" Her father's voice blasted up the hallway with an urgency she'd never heard before.

She bolted off the bed and ran up the hall. The beeping grew louder, then stopped.

It wasn't an alarm clock.

It was the perimeter alarm.

She hit the hardwood in the office so quickly her socked feet slipped and she had to grab the desk to keep her balance.

Her father stood in front of his computer, watching the monitor.

Where was Ian? Had he not heard her father? "What's wrong?"

Looking over his shoulder, her dad frowned, his eyebrows knit together. "You need to see this."

Even as she crossed the room, she knew. The perimeter alarm. Ian's absence.

He was running. The realization left her numb. "How did he get out?"

"He used Zane's code. Must have seen it when you left yesterday. The alarm went off because he entered it wrong the first two times."

By the time she joined her father at the monitor, a dark sedan was pulling away from the main gate. She didn't have to ask to know that Ian was in it. "Roll it back."

Her father straightened and braced his hands on his hips. "Mak, I know how this looks. He—"

"Roll it back." She ground the words out through gritted teeth. What was Ian thinking? How dare her father defend him?

Maybe he'd seen something she'd missed on the laptop. Maybe he'd been toying with her all along, waiting to get access.

Maybe she'd been used. Again.

Her father fiddled with the keyboard, then stepped aside. "Press the space bar when you're ready." He sounded almost defeated, but by Ian? Or by her refusal to hear him out?

Makenzie eased around him to stand directly in front of the screen. Déjà vu overwhelmed her. Hadn't she just done this very thing, but with Ian by her side?

Now he was gone. She pressed the space bar slowly, half hoping it wouldn't show what she suspected.

The camera focused on the main gate.

Ian appeared, jogging to the interior code box. He looked at the camera and keyed in a code. It was the wrong one because he stopped, looked at the camera again and punched the keys a second time, then a third.

He stepped through the gate as the sedan glided up.

Makenzie punched the space bar, the image frozen on Ian as he slid into the back of the same vehicle they'd seen on video at the castle. Her jaw tightened with nausea, but she forced the feeling aside and stepped into the role she should have taken all along. Unattached investigator. "What codes did he enter the first two times?"

Easing her aside, her father closed the offending video screen and pulled up another window. "The gate is a six-digit code then the pound sign to enter. He entered five digits before hitting Pound. 87878 both times. That's not an error entering Zane's code. Zane's was 936524."

Ian had purposely entered a fake number

and had purposely repeated it. "Why would he do that?"

"I know you don't want to hear this, but it's likely some sort of message." He held up his hand and pulled the video feed up again, rewinding it to when Ian first appeared. "Watch him. He looks at the camera. Enters the code, and looks again. I think he knew a bad code would alert me."

It was possible. Makenzie leaned closer to the screen. Ian didn't look angry or determined. He looked...sad? She straightened and crossed her arms. "Why would he run without talking to me? Why would he get into a vehicle with the person who likely wants both of us dead?"

"I think you know the answer to that one." Her father wrapped an arm around her shoulder and pulled her close. "Same reason I would. Same reason you would."

"To protect me." Shaking her head, she pulled away from him. The last thing she needed was to get lost in emotions now. "I don't know. I trusted him professionally enough to let him see those laptops, and he did this." She dragged her hand down her face and turned from the screen. She'd been ready to hand him her heart again as well. "I have to call the commander now. I can't hide any longer. He's a fugitive again."

"Is he?" Her father's voice raised as though he was amused.

She whirled on him. "Nothing about this is funny."

"I never said it was." Yet he wore a slight smile. "I know why he entered that particular code. He's smart, Mak. I think he has his memory again."

Her jaw slacked. "Why would you say that?"

"Two reasons. From past visits, he knew it would take two blown codes to trip the alarm. Unless you let that slip, he hasn't been told that in the past couple of days."

While she'd mentioned in brief what her father's security looked like, she hadn't gone into detail. "What's the other reason?"

"Did you tell him what I used to do with the CIA? What type of analysis I did?" When she shook her head, he let a full smile escape, then navigated to a search engine and brought up a diagram of a phone keypad. "This is Cryptography 101. The keypad has letters on it, like a telephone. Mack, I think he spelled something. That's why the code was too short." He opened another window and started typing.

"No, he repeated two numbers. That's not a code. That's random." This was foolishness. She reached for the desk phone.

No more hiding. With Ian on the run, it was time to take her chances with a mole in her team.

Her father stopped what he was doing and lightly grasped her wrist. "Trust me."

"You're about the only person I trust anymore." She muttered the words, wrestling the heartache into place. What did it say about her that she'd been duped *again*?

"Not me. Ian." Her dad stepped away from the screen and pointed to a list of nonsense phrases. "I put the numbers into a website that generates words from phone numbers. Look at the third one."

Makenzie rolled her eyes but obeyed. This was—

Her eyes landed on the words.

Trust me.

Reaching around her father, she swiped the mouse and reopened the video screen, staring at Ian's upturned face.

Trust me.

Did she dare?

The hope sending electric pulses through her veins said she desperately wanted to.

"I don't even know how to find him." She stalked around the desk and stood in front of the closed curtains, almost afraid she'd be eye to eye with a drone if she peeked out into the evening sky. "I've managed to get my cover blown on a major undercover op and to lose a man who is essentially a fugitive. If I have a job when this is over, it will only be because God intervened." Trusting Ian might have cost her everything. "When I call this in, that will be it for me. Especially since I'm the one who lost him."

"Did you really lose him?" Her father handed her his phone.

A map showed a dot moving down the mountain, headed toward Asheville.

Was that—? "How?"

"You think I wasn't going to have a way to track him? I trusted him...to a point. I loaned him the shirt he's wearing."

Makenzie's fingers tightened around the phone. If she wasn't trying to keep her head squarely in the professional realm, she'd hug her dad right now. "You tagged the shirt."

"There's a tracker in the hem."

God bless her father. "I need your car and any gear you have." She would call this in once she got moving. With Ian in that car, hiding their location was no longer a priority. Ian might already know who the mole was.

No, she could no longer do this on her own because, if Ian had recovered his memory and was on the move, then something was about to go down.

"There's a go bag in the bottom of the coat closet." Her dad shut off the computer and moved to follow. "I'm coming with you."

Holding a hand up between them, she halted his forward momentum. "No. You're not. I'm calling in my team. I'm not rushing in by myself. I'll pull surveillance until they arrive. That's all." When he started to argue, she rested her hand on his shoulder. "Dad, I know you're worried, but this is what I do, and it has to be by the book. All of it. No civilians."

"I'm not good at being a civilian, you know." Her father pulled her close and pressed a kiss to her forehead. "I'm definitely not good at watching my little girl run headfirst into danger."

"I know."

"I'll be praying."

"I know that, too." She stretched up on tiptoes to kiss his cheek then took off at a run to secure the laptops in the safe and gear up.

Ian's future, and hers, would be determined in the next few hours.

She just prayed they survived.

* * *

Less than an hour later, the blip on the map stopped moving on a dead-end road outside the town of Black Mountain.

As she'd hit the road, Makenzie had alerted the team out of Camp McGee, the main headquarters for Eagle Overwatch. She'd given little detail about the past few days, had merely said she'd located Ian and believed she had an arms dealer named Storm in her sights.

Led by Alex "Rich" Richardson, the team had geared up and was headed her way. She updated them on Ian's current location.

Roger. ETA forty-five minutes.

She had no lights and sirens to allow her to get to Ian faster, and she didn't dare go much over the speed limit with cars slowing for the weather and the roads growing slicker by the second. The snow that had started as a gentle flurry now poured in a wind-driven near whiteout.

Makenzie kneaded the steering wheel

until her hands felt raw, but she couldn't settle. Couldn't even pray. Tonight would finally provide answers. Whatever Ian was doing, the world would know soon if he was innocent or guilty.

This night could end both of their careers and any hope of a future together... If he still wanted one.

If she did. Knowing the truth could change everything.

Fifteen minutes later, at a bend in the road, she pulled the SUV onto a back road and studied the landscape. To her right, the path Ian had followed was little more than a gravel drive that wound up the mountain. Glancing at the phone, she figured Ian was about a quarter of a mile up.

The team would move faster with intel, and the only way to get it was for her to ascend the mountain without being seen.

She'd have to hike it, sticking to the woods along the road for cover. Pulling on her black coat, she grabbed her dad's backpack and hefted it onto her shoulders,

checked the ammo in her sidearm and holstered it.

This was what she was built for. Action.
Movement. She'd recon the situation at the
top, contact the team then wait for them to
bring in backup.

However this went down, it ended tonight.

With the sun long set, the temperature
bottomed out quickly. Makenzie kept to
the tree line off of the main road, trying to
avoid cameras, people or vehicles. It was
freezing in the woods, but at least the snow
and wind were blocked.

So was nearly any source of light. She
kept her head down, planting her feet carefully, listening for anything that could in-
dicate trouble.

She was pretty sure her feet were about to
freeze when the first lights broke through
the trees. Makenzie slowed, glancing at her
watch. The team still had nearly half an
hour.

Stashing the backpack behind a stump,

she pocketed her father's silenced phone and crept to the edge of the trees, keeping low.

A small cabin sat in the center of the clearing with all of the lights blazing. Looked like it had been used for hunting or a weekend getaway. It was older, off the beaten path and nondescript. The perfect hideout.

Somehow, though, she'd assumed Storm would think like Butler. Bigger. Better. Flashier.

But no. Smaller. Quieter. Darker. Those were the things that had allowed Storm to hide while Butler wore the target as the face of the organization.

Nobody moved around the cabin. The only motion came from the swirling snow, which fell heavier where the trees were thinner. The snow dampened sound, leaving only the peaceful swish of it falling through the trees. Normally, she loved that sound. Tonight, it seemed to hide danger.

A dark green SUV sat close to the porch, facing down the driveway, primed for a fast getaway. The sedan that had picked up Ian sat beside it.

Makenzie's heart picked up speed. He was here. *Lord, please... Please let him be innocent. Please let this be the end of the bad and not the beginning of worse.* Makenzie wrestled her emotions into check. If the worst happened, she had to respond as an investigator, not as a woman in love.

She drew her sidearm and scanned the area, then eased her way toward the vehicles. Crouching as she circled them, she lifted her head only enough to inspect the interiors.

Clear.

Keeping low, she moved to the side of the house, skirting the floodlights, and crept to a window. The hum of voices drifted out, but they were too low to discern tone or words. One was a male. One was a female.

Makenzie pressed against the rough logs and eased closer to peek in the window.

Ian stood facing her, his face tight, as a woman with dark hair spoke to him with animated hand motions.

Familiarity jolted through Makenzie. The woman's posture. Her hair. The way she moved her hands when she spoke. It reminded her of—

The woman turned and stalked away from Ian toward the front door, her profile in plain view.

Audra.

Makenzie gasped, then clamped her teeth into her lower lip, praying no one had heard. Her heart hammered so hard she could see the beat in the dark spots before her eyes.

She would not pass out. Could not pass out.

She fought the shock to her system and tried to breathe normally, tried to piece together what she saw with what she knew.

Audra was alive. Living and breathing and talking to Ian.

Makenzie's eyes squeezed shut as she tried to regain her equilibrium. *How?* What was—

A twig cracked. Cold steel pressed against the back of her neck. The world snapped into focus.

It was too late. The gun barrel dug deeper into her flesh, bruising at the base of her skull.

"Put down the gun. We're going inside."

SEVENTEEN

A voice by the window drew Ian's glance, but he brought his attention to Audra.

She was the real threat. If he didn't convince her of his loyalty soon, she would put a bullet in his head and move on.

The fact that she hadn't already was a clear indication that she was desperate, that she had no one else who could do his job.

In the half hour since Ian had been unceremoniously ushered into the house, Audra had been less than the cold, calculated killer he'd been investigating for nearly four years. She prowled the room, eyeing him with suspicion, clearly second-guessing every choice she'd made since the day she *became* the dark side. She stalked toward the window, her fists balled at her sides. "I should have killed you instead of bringing you here."

This was more than a fight for the investigation. It was a fight for his life.

"If you wanted me dead, I'd be dead. You need me." He blinked slowly, putting on an air of annoyed arrogance. He crossed his arms and eyed her from head to toe, sizing her up. He also tried his best to ignore the two bouncers she'd stationed by the door. They looked like street fighters from a back alley gym. Angry and mean. "Considering you gave Robert Butler the order to have me killed, maybe I should strike first."

"Is that a threat?"

"A threat? You had me poisoned. Marked me for death. Shot at me. I think a threat is mild compared to that." He stepped toward her, squaring his shoulders, attempting to look more menacing than he felt. "You vetted me for three years. Put me through my paces for the past year, had me hacking ridiculously easy systems... It's not like you to assume I'd turned on you just because Robert Butler was foolish enough to hire an undercover agent. I had no idea Makenzie was Butler's number two. You should have kept a tighter rein on him." He'd assumed Overwatch's investigation would be scrapped with his disappearance. There had been no indication that Storm was tied to Butler. When the FBI asked him to do a deep dive on Storm and a possible link to Audra, there had been no connection between the two arms dealers. This was why interagency communications needed to stop bowing to chest-thumping pride that held intel too close to the vest. Working together would have wrapped this all up before danger reared its head.

That could wait for debrief. Right now, he had to save his skin...and Makenzie's. "Makenzie was your partner once." Ian narrowed his eyes. "Maybe you're setting *me* up?" He towered over her. "Maybe the government helped you fake your death. Maybe I was partnered with Makenzie because she was investigating me." It had actually been the other way around. Makenzie had been suspected of being a part of Audra's scheme until Ian had cleared her. "Maybe you've been gathering intel on my black-hat hacking for years." Intel the FBI had planted for her to find.

"You've gotten cozy with Fuller the past few days, not reaching out. Not making sure she was out of the way." She moved so fast Ian could hardly track her, but the next thing he knew, a Sig was pressed against his abdomen. "I should have piloted that drone myself. I wouldn't have missed."

How he managed not to flinch, he'd never know. "Those days got me access to the laptop *you* trusted Butler with."

Doubt flittered across Audra's face. While she didn't move the gun, the pressure against his diaphragm eased. "And?"

"It's been erased. Fuller's intel is gone."

Audra holstered her pistol. "Prove it."

"The next time Fuller opens that laptop, yours will alert. I can remote access it and show you a blank hard drive." Hopefully, Makenzie was on the way with reinforcements. It was a big risk, hoping her father would figure out his signal.

Regardless, she'd find him. He'd discovered the tracker in his borrowed shirt thirty seconds after he put it on.

His handler hadn't given him clearance to read her into the mission. The FBI didn't trust someone who'd been working within Butler's organization when the chance to take Storm down was within reach.

It would take the FBI two hours to arrive. The team at Camp McGee could be here in less than one.

They'd think he was the bad guy. The FBI had cast more than enough suspicion on him to leave him with a broken reputation. Hopefully he could come clean tonight.

Maybe Makenzie would forgive him and he could tell her he'd never stopped loving her.

Maybe she wouldn't.

He couldn't flinch at the pain that scenario brought. Not if they were going to survive. "Will you finally tell me what it is you think only I can hack for you? Pretty sure I've proved my loyalty."

Audra drummed her fingers on her hips

as though deciding whether to trust him. Finally, she walked around him to the laptop on the table. "It involves NATO."

NATO. She was after bigger scores than machine guns.

Something thumped on the porch, and Audra tipped her head toward the sound. "You two. Outside."

The door guards obeyed.

"Too many ears means more cleanup later." Audra opened the laptop.

Cleanup. She'd likely kill everyone involved once she had what she wanted. Even him. That was one good way to keep her secret, by recruiting new talent and wasting the old every couple of years.

"We've been hitting individual bases and picking up weapons where we can," she said as Ian stopped beside her. "I want to go bigger."

"You mean nuclear." Access to the right NATO databases could give her shipping routes, stockpiles... The very thing top officials feared and fought.

Another thud came from outside.

Lord, don't let that be Makenzie. The image of her limp body being dragged over the wide boards of the old porch was enough to drop him.

Audra drew her weapon and faced the entry.

Bouncer Number One shoved the door open. Makenzie stumbled in after him, dropping to one knee as another guard pushed her from behind.

He kept his face impassive and his feet in place, although he wanted to dive in and shield her from Audra's wrath.

Makenzie didn't even look at him. From where she crouched on the floor, she fixed her gaze on Audra, eyes wide with shock. "What—?" It was as though her brain shut down at the sight of her mentor, partner and friend.

A traitor.

He should have fought harder to read her in. The fact that Audra was alive had clearly rocked her. Shock was likely the reason she'd been caught.

Ian couldn't move a finger to rescue her. Yet. *Lord, don't let Audra pull the trigger.*

Audra holstered her weapon and dropped to her knees in front of Makenzie. "Mak." She wrapped her arms around Makenzie in the kind of hug that a mother would give.

Ian wanted to rip the two women apart. Audra was playing Makenzie. He could see the plan forming. She was buying time, pretending to be sympathetic and undercover.

She was playing on Makenzie's pain.

Audra was smart. If she killed Makenzie outright, it would set Overwatch onto her trail with focused vengeance.

If she convinced Makenzie she worked for the government, Mak might let her walk.

Ian balled his fists, trying to formulate a plan.

Makenzie hesitated, her arms at her sides, but tears stood in her eyes when they met his over Audra's shoulder.

He shook his head once, slightly. *Don't buy it. She'll kill you.*

Her eyebrows furrowed and she turned

away, slowly hugging Audra. "I saw your body…"

Ian ached with tension. Makenzie was in pain and in danger. He wanted to fight for her, warn her…

But he was outnumbered and had to watch her fall for a killer's lies.

Audra stood and helped Makenzie to stand. "I was pulled undercover to investigate a mole in the unit. Overwatch faked my death and set me up as Storm, working the European arm of Butler's organization."

Lies. Ian tried to catch Makenzie's eye, but she watched Audra, still stunned by her former partner's apparent rise from the grave. *Mak, look at me.*

Makenzie glanced over her shoulder at the men by the door. She walked away from them toward the kitchen, dragging her hands down her cheeks. "I don't…" When she turned to Audra, she carefully avoided looking at Ian. "Why is he here?"

Audra's expression hardened. She glanced at Ian and her hand went to her hip, where she'd holstered her gun.

He couldn't help taking a step back, searching for cover.

She would shoot him to save herself. Claim he was the mole and escape before Overwatch or the FBI arrived.

Leaving Makenzie to think he'd lied all along.

Makenzie stepped to Audra's side. She glanced at the door, and one of Audra's lackeys followed her gaze.

"Mak..." Ian's voice was sharp. "She's lying."

Audra whirled toward him and reached for her sidearm.

The room offered nowhere to hide.

He darted a look to Makenzie. The only way he survived was if she took action on his behalf before Audra could fire.

That would mean she chose to trust him over Audra.

Audra ripped the pistol from its holster and took aim at Ian.

Makenzie leaped. She tackled Audra, shoving her into one of the guards. The gun clattered to the floor.

Ian dove for the pistol and aimed at the guard as Makenzie pinned Audra facedown to the floor. "FBI. Lace your fingers behind your head."

Makenzie looked up at his command, eyes wide. She started to speak, but pounding on the porch steps silenced her.

The door burst open. An armed team breached the room, weapons drawn. "Federal agents!"

The shouts were everywhere, all at once.

One of the men leveled a rifle on Ian. "Ian Andrews. On your face. Now." He knew that voice. Had worked with Alex "Rich" Richardson on a case out of Fort Bragg.

For now, he didn't try to defend himself. This would sort out as soon as he reached Camp McGee and his FBI handler vouched for him. He obeyed the order, laying Audra's pistol on the ground and lying facedown. He winced as Rich jerked his hands behind his back and cuffed him like the criminal everyone in Overwatch thought he was.

Everyone except Makenzie.

A lot was about to happen. She'd have to answer for her silence the past few days and work through her intel with Overwatch. He'd have to go to Washington, DC, to turn over evidence and debrief his year undercover.

She'd have to forgive him for disappearing on a mission without saying goodbye. Doing so after they'd confessed their feelings for one another must have cut her deeply.

He'd never be able to say he was sorry enough.

As Rich walked him to the door, he dug his feet in when they reached Makenzie. They could be separated for weeks, and he wasn't leaving here without giving her something in return for the pain his mission had caused.

Rich stopped walking, though his grip on Ian's biceps held fast.

Ian scanned Makenzie's face. What he wouldn't give—

He opted for words over actions. For

now. "Mak, I remember you. I remember all of it."

"I know."

"Let's go, Andrews." Rich tugged at his arm, drawing him toward the door as Makenzie watched, her expression grim.

When she learned the truth, would she forgive him?

Makenzie leaned against the rough railing of the dock that ran along the orchard pond and breathed in the Christmas-scented air. Snow flurries whirled around her, promising a rare second storm during the night. Remnants of the snowfall that had dogged her as she chased Ian clung to the shadows.

Christmas Day.

She'd spent the morning watching Noah tear into gifts under the Christmas tree, then she'd attempted to score a goal on him as he guarded the new soccer net in the backyard.

It had felt good to dribble a ball between her feet. To give her nephew pointers and to share his enthusiasm for the game she'd once loved.

Maybe she could love it again.

Leaning over the railing, she stared into the water that reflected clouds, as snowflakes drifted gently to the surface. The orchard was silent, save the soft shushing sound of snow falling through fir needles. Today, she felt sort of clean and fresh, like new snow.

For too long, she'd walled up parts of herself behind betrayal and pain, walking in a cynicism that stopped her from trusting everyone.

Even God.

That had changed in a backwoods cabin, faced with the shock of Audra's reappearance and the decision to trust Ian.

The decision to trust herself. That was what it had really boiled down to. Because of Coach Davies, she'd stopped trusting her instincts and the answers to her prayers. Had run with the idea that, given time, everyone would betray her.

Audra had.

Ian hadn't.

The walls had been at work when he'd vanished, so she hadn't considered there might be a very good reason.

Like the FBI had been suspicious of Audra for years, until she'd died. Makenzie's transfer to Maryland was so that she could be surveilled by Overwatch.

Ian had cleared her a year into their partnership, then asked to remain by her side. Now he was gone again. He hadn't reached out as she'd expected him to after their brief encounter as Rich led him away and after she'd learned the truth about his year undercover. He was likely still in DC, buried in debriefings and interviews as the FBI built a solid case against Audra.

The FBI. When it had become clear that someone in Overwatch was dirty, they'd stepped in to investigate from the outside. Ironic, considering that's what Overwatch was tasked to do within the Army. As evidence grew that there was a link between Audra and a new dealer named Storm who was rising in Europe, Gage had been sent to investigate while Ian was partnered with Makenzie to make sure she wasn't involved.

He'd cleared her but had asked to stay on as her partner. When Audra had begun to build a team, the FBI saw a chance to put Ian into her good graces. He allowed himself to appear like a black hat hacker who'd turned on his country in order to win Audra's trust.

No one had realized that Audra was joining forces with the very dealer that Overwatch was already investigating. Not even Ian. Until it was too late. When Audra spotted Makenzie in Butler's organization, she assumed that Ian was working with her as well, blowing up both investigations.

But Makenzie and Ian had done enough to take her down.

Overwatch had catalogued Makenzie's evidence and debriefed her, then sent her home for a week of leave to detox her undercover persona. She'd return next week to wrap up details so Overwatch and the FBI could put their heads together and dragnet the rest of Storm's organization.

If only the FBI and Overwatch had communicated all along. While Overwatch had chased Butler and his contacts within military bases, the FBI had been tracking Storm, who was overseas building a network of buyers. Putting their heads together would have completed a picture that might have shortened the investigation and prevented the attack that left Ian's memory in pieces.

Instead, Makenzie had gone in alone to investigate Butler because the FBI had decided it was time to put a years-long plan into place and to bring him face-to-face with Audra, who'd been courting him for years. The FBI had built an evidence trail to make Ian look money-hungry and bitter, ripe for the picking.

Before she'd faked her death, Audra had gathered all of the intel she could on Overwatch, intending to sell it to the highest bidder. That list included safe houses. There had been no mole, just a greedy, conniving "dead" agent using the system against them.

Now all of that was over. She wanted to talk to Ian. Had the emotions she'd seen on his face as Rich had taken him into custody been true? He remembered her— remembered them—but had a year changed them too much to go back to where they'd started?

"Mak."

Makenzie lifted her head and gripped the railing tighter. Her imagination had sounded a little bit too real. Counting to three to steel herself against disappointment, she let go of the rail and turned around.

Ian stood about ten feet away, at the end of the dock. He wore jeans and a hunter green sweater. Snow clung to his hair. He had his hands shoved in his pockets and he was just…watching.

The irrational, silly part of her wanted to hurl herself down the dock and throw herself at him. The rational, tactical part of her urged caution. He might not accept her embrace. He could be here to tell her that a year apart had changed everything. She leaned against the railing, seeking something solid.

He took one step closer, his gaze never leaving hers. "You didn't believe Audra."

Makenzie shook her head. She'd known the truth from digging into the emails on Butler's laptop. Storm had pulled the strings. Audra's story had been a lie from the moment she opened her mouth. That hug…it had been designed to play on her broken emotions and to manipulate her fears.

She swallowed the anger that tried to twist its way up. This wasn't about Audra. It was about her. And Ian. "You would never use my past pain against me." It had all grown clear in that moment, as they'd locked gazes over Audra's shoulder. While she didn't yet know why he'd left, she'd known without a doubt that he'd never intended to hurt her.

"I wouldn't." His voice was low, husky. He stepped toward her again and still, his eyes never left hers. He raised the slightest smile. "It's been a long year."

"Longer than you know." A year of being someone else. Of wondering where he was and why he'd left. Of hardening her heart until it had finally cracked and she'd been forced to trust her God.

And Ian.

"I think I know exactly how long it's been." As though the rubber band that had been holding him snapped, he closed the space between them and placed his hands on the railing on either side of her, looking down into her eyes. "I missed you."

"I was mad at you." Even though she knew the truth now, she needed to say it. If they were going to start fresh—and she desperately hoped they were—then they needed to lay the past to rest.

His head tilted. He reached up and slipped a loose strand of hair behind her ear, letting his knuckles trail down her cheek. "I deserved it." He lifted her chin so that she looked him straight in the eye. "As long as we're being honest, you need to know that it killed me to wonder what you were thinking. Every day I was gone, I knew you were hating me. Believing I'd betrayed you. I knew it had ripped open a wound and there was nothing I could do to fix it."

She hadn't considered it from his angle. Pulled undercover, he'd had no way to prepare the people he loved. No way to reach out to them. You just did your job and hoped for the best. If he felt about her the way he'd once promised, then his pain must have rivaled her own. Resting her hands on his chest, she tried to read his expression, to see what he was thinking about where this was going.

Although it didn't take a tactical brain to figure out that it was going somewhere very good if he was standing this close to her. "So what happens now?"

Sliding his hand from her chin to her shoulder, he looked over her. "Now? I'm not interested in field work anymore."

"Me neither." The entire ordeal had left her weary, ready for something that didn't involve the darkest side of humanity.

"So, would you be interested in…a whole new way of life?" When his gaze dropped to hers, it was the old Ian looking at her. The one of laughter and teasing and love.

"Depends. What are you thinking?"

"I know a guy who runs a tree farm. He's interested in passing it along in a few years to somebody who wants a change of pace."

"Really?" Her dad had never said a word, but she knew the farm held his heart, and he wanted it to continue growing.

"He wants to keep it in the family though. Told me a few minutes ago that his daughter might be interested, but he'd like her to have a partner."

When his gaze dropped to hers, her heartbeat picked up the pace. "What kind of partner?" She wrapped her fingers in the front of his sweater and pulled him closer. "A business partner?"

Every ounce of amusement fled his expression. "A lifelong partner." His eyes roamed her face, searching for an answer.

Makenzie stood on tiptoes, putting herself eye to eye with him, so close she could feel the warmth of his breath on her lips. "I think she'd like that."

This time, when he kissed her, it was without hesitation. He knew her. Knew her good days and her bad days. Knew her hopes and her fears. They would need to get to know each other again, with all of the experiences of the past year blended in between them, but of one thing she had no doubt...

As he slipped his arms around her waist and pulled her closer, she knew. Ian would guard her heart and her trust with his life. And she'd do the same for him.

* * * * *

If you enjoyed this story, please look for these other books by Jodie Bailey:

Captured at Christmas
Witness in Peril
Defending from Danger

Dear Reader,

When I first started Ian and Makenzie's story, I thought it was about trust, but I realized it was about the verse Ian reads in the safe house. God is the God who sees us. At our lowest, our darkest, our loneliest... God sees us.

Ian lost the knowledge of who he was. Makenzie and Ian both struggled with the truth about him. But Makenzie's father? He always knew. He took precautions, but he never doubted Ian's core identity. He saw what Ian couldn't see in himself.

That's God. We lose our way and forget we belong to God and our identity is in Him. Like Ian "falling into a black hole," we feel alone and scared. Or, like Makenzie, we believe we're a mess because we don't measure up to someone else. But God sees into the deepest parts of who we are. He knows. He loves.

He sends others to love us. When I was in high school, lost in my own black hole, God sent a teacher who saw me and recognized that a writer lived in me alongside a little girl who needed acceptance. Through her, God saw me. Encouraged me. Loved me. Thirty years later, she's still a part of my life.

Never forget *God sees and God loves,* even when it feels hopeless. Oh, I pray that sinks into your soul.

I hope you enjoyed Makenzie and Ian's story. You can drop by jodiebailey.com to find ways to get in touch and to see what's next. Thanks for spending your precious time here. I appreciate that more than you know!

Jodie Bailey